Interesting
Monsters

Interesting Monsters

FICTIONS

Aldo Alvarez

Graywolf Press

SAINT PAUL, MINNESOTA

MAR _ 4 2002

Copyright © 2001 by Aldo Alvarez

Publication of this volume is made possible in part by a grant provided by the Minnesota State Arts Board through an appropriation
by the Minnesota State Legislature, and by a grant from the National Endowment for the Arts. Significant support has also been
provided by the Bush Foundation; Dayton's Project Imagine with
support from Target Foundation; the McKnight Foundation; a
Grant made on behalf of the Stargazer Foundation; and other gener-
ous contributions from foundations, corporations, and individuals.
To these organizations and individuals we offer our heartfelt thanks.

Published by Graywolf Press
2402 University Avenue, Suite 203
Saint Paul, Minnesota 55114
All rights reserved.

www.graywolfpress.org

Published in the United States of America

ISBN 1-55597-356-6

2 4 6 8 9 7 5 3 1
First Graywolf Printing, 2001

Library of Congress Control Number: 2001088673

Cover design: Scott Sorenson

Cover photograph: Plastock, *Figure of Man in Pink Suit* ©Photonica

Acknowledgments

"Heat Rises," originally published in *Christopher Street,* September 1994.

"Index Card, Index Finger," originally published in *ARK/ Angel Review,* January 1994.

"A Small Indulgence," originally published in *The Blue Moon Review/Blue Penny Quarterly,* March 1996.

"Quintessence," originally published in *Harrington Gay Men's Fiction Quarterly,* Fall 2000.

"Ghosts, Pockets, Traces, Necessary Clouds," originally published in *Pen & Sword,* July 1995; reprinted in *Best American Gay Fiction 1,* August 1996 (Little, Brown).

"Losing Count," originally published in *Tatlin's Tower,* September 2000.

"Property Values," originally published in *Pen & Sword,* April 1995; reprinted in *A & U Magazine,* April 1999.

"Flatware," originally published in *A & U Magazine,* April 1997.

"Rog & Venus Become an Item," originally published in *Psychotrain,* January 1994.

"Up Close," originally published in *I See Gays,* April 2000.

"Death by Bricolage," originally published in *GayPlace Online Magazine,* November 1996; reprinted in *Contra/Dictions: New Queer Male Fiction,* October 1998 (Arsenal Pulp Press).

"Ephemera," originally published in *Amelia Magazine,* March 1997.

"Fixing a Shadow," originally published in *A & U Magazine,* August 1996.

for
Doña Luz Alaida de Álvarez
(aka Luja, Luchía, Mami)
(1930–1999)

Contents

*Interesting
Monsters*

Heat Rises

i.

Mark lined the walls of the attic with fibrous, wavy-textured gray padding. His body was covered in sweat; not only did the material keep the room soundproof, it kept heat in. He took off his shirt. He flipped the switch on a rickety old fan and stood in front of it, hoping to dry off. The fan whirred and hummed and clicked rhythmically, and he closed his eyes to let the sound into his ears. He could hear the curve of the sound as it wavered slightly on and off its own strange key, as if it were a shape against the palm of his hand. The hum persisted in his head later on, when Mark and his mother had sandwiches for lunch on the porch. He did not know what the hum said to him, but it was something he was willing to contemplate.

ii.

Josie had been surprised to see her grown-up son come home without even a phone call. That wasn't like Mark; or, at least, not the Mark of recent memory. The Mark of fifteen years ago, yes, he would appear on her doorstep whenever he felt like it. The Mark of recent memory called before he came home—or, most likely, called to say that he couldn't. Or wouldn't.

"Hi, Mom. . . ." This said by Mark with the least apparent enthusiasm.

Mark stood there with his duffel bag, a baseball cap turned backwards, a black shirt missing one button, old sneakers, one shoelace untied.

"Back from baseball practice?" Josie asked.

"No," Mark said. "I'd like to stay for a while, if I may."

"Yes, you may," Josie said.

They hugged, and Mark took his mom under his arm and walked her into the house.

"I heard one of your old songs on the radio the other day," Josie said. "Do you get paid for that still?"

"Yeah, but not as much as I used to. Anyway, I still get a cut from the stuff I produce for other people."

"At least you can feed yourself," she said. "How's the girlfriend?" Whoever she was. . . .

"*What* girlfriend?"

"Touchy, touchy," Josie said.

At that moment, mother and son renewed the contract under whose conditions the subject Girlfriend, and all the derivations thereof ("When are you going to get married?" "When am I going to meet her?" "I'd like to see my grandchildren before I die"), became a Subject Not To Be Discussed.

When a truck arrived half an hour later, Josie knew the visit was for a long haul. Movers brought in his studio equipment, synthesizer banks, keyboards and their stands, and other music paraphernalia described in Josie's parlance as junk. Her son, the ex-pop star and record producer, was moving back into the old house for reasons not yet known to her, maybe . . . girlfriend related? And, at forty years old, Mark wouldn't be doing things lightly. It all smacked of a midlife crisis. In any case, Josie wondered if it was her fault that Mark carried all that junk with him, if she shouldn't have brought him that solder-it-yourself, rinky-dink synthesizer kit from England at an impressionable age.

"Can I put my stuff in Dad's office while I fix up the attic?" he asked.

"I don't think he'd mind," she said. Not that he'd complain from the grave.

"I was asking about you."

"No, go ahead."

"Are you really sure?"

"No, I think it's a terrific idea. Actually, why don't you use the office instead? I'm hardly ever there."

"The attic's more private." It had also been his personal den since anyone could remember. "Besides, I'm going to clean it up and soundproof it. It's going to be a lot easier to do that upstairs."

"Isn't it awfully hot up there?"

"Yeah. But I'll set up a small air conditioner in the window. Don't worry about the utilities. I'll pay them."

Once he had the studio running, the utilities bill suggested to Josie that the watt-usage level of his production suite could light and heat and microwave a small country. But Mark footed the bill, and all was well between mother and son in that department.

iii.

Rosalie, Josie's neighbor, watched from her kitchen window a parade of equipment which, had she not been familiar with the high-tech look that everyday kitchen appliances were taking, would have looked like her neighbor had suddenly taken up atom-bomb building as a hobby. But this wasn't necessarily what she paid most attention to. It was Mark, joining in with the movers to haul all that stuff into the house. She thought he looked like a nerdier version of one of the pirates in her FlowerSword romances, and his shirt was quite nearly open to that brave, valiant, so-near-the-belly-button point which signified to her, like a ringing bell, that it was time to moisten. Not that she was devoid of ironic distance; she just liked to pretend she was ready to be swept away. She secretly hoped it would happen, though she was pretty sure they wouldn't allow her two young children onto pirate ships of the kind her consort would command.

In any case, Rosalie waited a few days to attempt to approach him. Her curiosity, piqued by the banging and shuffling she heard coming from the attic of Josie's house, drew her to insinuate herself into Josie's kitchen. Josie had once spoken about her very successful son in the music business. Might he be her pirate?

"Yeah, that's my son, all right," Josie said. "He'll be staying here for some time, I take it."

"May I meet him?"

"You've got a good chance to see him around the house. To be honest, he's not quick to ask for dates, or speak for more than five minutes. And I wouldn't impose on him, at his age, by introducing him to someone I approve of. I'm sad to say that I've given up. I don't know what his problem with women is. . . ."

"Oh, well," Rosalie said. "I guess I'll wait for the right moment to meet him."

"I'm sure that you can get his attention, if he ever leaves that attic."

Rosalie felt very determined, very beautiful, very sexy, and *vivid*.

iv.

Mark lugged the five-foot-long, rusty fish tank from his bedroom up to the attic. He put the fish tank on top of two cement blocks. He attached mattress springs to the bottom of a small vacuum-tube guitar amplifier that produced warm, deep, fuzzy sounds no matter what was plugged into it. He put the spring-mounted amp inside the tank, backed up against a corner. At the opposite corner, he placed a microphone.

He played back a recording of the fan's hum through the amp. The amplifier vibrated on its springs, giving the hum a slow twang, the fish tank adding echo. Mark re-recorded the whole thing several times, varying the volume and the bass and treble settings on the amp, and then listened to it through headphones.

He heard his soul, wavering, inside an empty room.

V.

Kip knew that Mark had asked him not to call him at home. But when fate offered the opportunity to produce the follow-up to a multi-platinum album by a band that claimed Mark as one of its influences, Kip, the engineer, the producer's sidekick, wasn't just going to turn it down right away. He'd attempt to coax his little producer friend into stepping up to the sound board.

"No," Mark said into the phone.

"Think of it for a minute," Kip said. "We're talking reputation-enhancing production chores. We're talking a big salary for you."

"I'm taken."

"Look, they worship you. They even like your difficult fourth album."

"I'm working on something."

"What's more important than the biggest break of your fuckin' dead career?"

OK, Kip thought, maybe I'm exaggerating the case.

"What I'm working on," Mark said.

"What."

"I want to know what my soul sounds like."

Kip knew that Mark was a bit on the unfathomable side, but this was five fathoms too deep.

"Are you serious?"

"Yeah. I'll let you listen to it when I'm done."

Kip hadn't heard him say anything so definite, so committed, so nearly polysyllabic, in some time.

"I take it it's important," Kip said.

"Yeah."

"Sure. I'll listen to it when you're done."

Anything for a friend, Kip thought.

vi.

Mark had made a six-minute tape of the hum, digitally processed, mixed and re-recorded into a form that deeply satisfied him. It was time to add other elements. He tried conventional drum-machine sounds, but they stuck out too much. He tried laying out a rhythm track from sampled snippets of the sound of phones being hung up on his answering machine, and that worked. He recorded the sound of a pencil's eraser thumping on a very sensitive mike. He modulated the sound and brought it down a few octaves, and played it in rhythm with the phone clicks, as a bass drum. He slapped and shook his old bottle-cap collection in its cigar box as if it were an African shaker. For a couple of weeks, he fiddled with the rhythm tracks until he was satisfied with the result.

vii.

After a period of watching her son go up to the attic, Josie couldn't quite get what he was up to, but she respected his privacy. She had to: he was nearly always up there when he wasn't in his bedroom. And if she tiptoed through the evil scientist's secret sanctum, her steps would be heard clear through the bedroom underneath it—and he who lived in that bedroom could easily guess who was poking around the corpses.

Little did she know that Mark had carpeted the floor. All that she saw or heard from him was what he cared to share with her. Lunchtimes, mostly. At night, when she was already in bed, he'd have something to eat after coming back home from wherever he rode off to in his car and then he'd spend late nights working in the attic. He'd sleep mornings and then have lunch and then work, or whatever it was that he did. That's all she knew. Eventually, she wanted to know more.

"So," she said, during another lunchtime on the porch, "what kind of monster are you building up there?"

"Nothing really specific yet," he said. "Trying to find my way into something."

"Oh yeah? Working on a record?"

"Not exactly."

"What it is then? Some new thing to make noise with?"

"It's part of it, but, no, that's not it."

Josie had forgotten how Mark requested the attention he needed by making her guess what the heck he was up to. He wouldn't hand out the information easily. It was like trying to cross the street with a very reticent animal, though you could manage with enough encouragement.

"I take it you're going to make me guess," she said.

"I don't know how to tell you," Mark said. "Or, I'm not sure if I can tell you."

"Why?"

"It's pretty weird."

"Tell me," Josie said, suddenly feeling very maternal and understanding.

"I'm working on my soul."

"*Don't* tell me," Josie said, suddenly feeling very maternal and misunderstanding.

"I told you you wouldn't want to hear it."

"Is this some musical kind of thing I don't know about?"

"No, Mom," Mark said. "I'm working on my soul. It must have a shape, a resonance, like the wave of a sound. I want to capture mine as sound and put it on tape."

As a young mother, she'd read all kinds of books about taking care of someone whose personality frightened you. Quiet, she could take. Talented, she could nurture. Weird, she could . . . she could hope to cope with.

"Is this for real, or are you just being pretentious for my benefit?" she asked.

"A bit of both," Mark said.

"Why?" she asked.

"I want to know what it sounds like."

viii.

Mark hooked up a hefty, roundheaded mike to a boom box. The boom box was as old and dated as its name: heavy and bulky, a garish silver console, manipulated by knobs and brusque, clunky mechanisms. He had a line out to the multi-track recorder and used an ambient mike to record the event from the air. He turned on the boom box, waved the mike. The boom box fed back on itself. It wailed and throbbed and screamed.

He played with this setup for a while until he gave it, with his performance, the range of expression of a master instrument.

He worked with several other elements to mix along the length of the piece. His mother's wedding silverware, falling on the old oak desk upstairs, slowed down to sound like bells. Two repeating loops of three-note cycles made by whistling into a tube played against itself with mesmeric effect. A tape of his breathing as he slept, spread out through the stereo image and amplified.

Two months had passed. He'd recorded all the sounds that he could see in his mind forming a whole, and he was satisfied. He was ready to work on the mix.

ix.

Rosalie had kept tabs on her neighbor's son, keeping track of his sightings as if she were compiling a UFO newsletter. They were few and far between, but they did stick in her mind. She was as intent on the outcome of the beard he was growing, which was sexy in a high-testosterone sort of way. Her kitchen window faced Josie's house; she had clear sight of the porch and often would sneak a peek at the Piper family at lunch. This morning, she had heard Josie's car drive away in an uncertain direction. Would he come out for lunch by himself on this very hot summer day and give her a chance to casually stroll up to him and say hi, away from motherly intervention?

Yes.

Mark came out lugging a huge radio-cassette player . He plugged it in, turned it on to a country and western station, went back in, and came back out with a sandwich and a big glass of iced tea. He sat on the floor, cross-legged.

The man on the porch was only wearing a pair of cutoff jeans and lumberjack boots. A chain hung from his neck. A bunch of rings dangled from the chain, one for each color of the rainbow.

Rosalie, unable to control herself, moistened.

Rosalie did not usually watch anyone eat with such force of intention. She'd watched her folks eat so as to gauge their appreciation of her; she watched her children eat to monitor their health. She watched Mark lift the sandwich to his mouth, the stringy muscles on his arms rising and falling; she watched him gulp his iced tea, his protuberant Adam's apple bobbing up and down; she watched him *munching.*

Soon enough, Mark Piper finished his noonday repast. Rosalie was too distraught by the whole spectacle to consider approaching him right then. But making him dinner would be a seriously good idea.

Mark turned to the tape player, turned off the radio, and ran a tape. She tried to listen closely to this man's taste in music.

A loud, woozy vibration started coming out of the radio. Mark closed his eyes.

The sound got into her head. Before she had a chance to notice, she was in an empty room.

An empty room, the floorboards quivering underneath her feet. Her husband leaving her. Balls of glass falling with dull but slowly dimming tones, breaking in slow motion. Realizing she could not ask anything from him, he was not coming back. Shaking, scratching sounds, a deep thud like falling meat. Her hands pulling open a plastic bath curtain, rushing out to see her husband come back to take her kids away from her—

She shook herself from the memory. It was too hard to take. She had trained herself not to think of things like that.

But the music insisted. A loud, fuzzy wail tearing through her heart, again.

She burst into tears. She looked at Mark, sitting quietly, eyes closed, listening to this music.

She wiped her face dry while trying to cover her ears. She left her house, conflicted from the swing of her feelings, her lack of control over them, and hardened, determined to stop them.

Mark opened his eyes, sensing her presence. She stood

before him, her hands over her ears, as if she were ready to scream her head off.

"Please turn that off," she said firmly. "That music is making me *think.*"

Mark laughed, then caught himself and stopped abruptly. She didn't find it funny.

Rosalie walked back home and shut herself in her bedroom.

Mark hadn't meant to disturb her.

He turned it down to a shallow whisper.

X.

As promised, Mark sent Kip a tape of his finished piece. Kip put it in the tape player, thinking, well, we can get some ideas out of this for future use, it's not all wasted time.

Once Kip was taken by this tune, he called his partner.

"What the *fuck* was *that*?" Kip asked.

"You didn't like it?"

"*Like* is not strong enough a word."

"So you liked it?"

"It's fuckin' fabulous, man!"

"No kidding?"

"I . . . I saw images, I felt things. . . it's the most amazing piece of music I've ever heard from you. It's like I've never heard you before. It was so beautiful, I cried like a fuckin' baby. And I'm *not* exaggerating. I played it over and over and over."

"Thank you," Mark said. Kip could hear him smiling shyly over the phone.

"Can you come up with a full album of this shit? I mean, the New Age or Ambient House thing's just ripe for the picking, with all the crud that's out there, and this is just going to blow them away! This could be huge—"

"No, Kip."

"And then film scores! I know a lot of music super-visors—"

"No, Kip, no."

"Whaddaya mean no? It's just *perfect*. You could do this for the rest of your life."

"Not what I want to do. It's my soul."

"Oh, no, don't get weird on me like that. If it's so pri-vate, why did you just give it to me?"

"I don't know," Mark said, "you might be able to talk me into releasing it. But not right now. I'm not sure it's something I want to do."

"You don't have to be," Kip said, "right now."

Their conversation shifted to tying up loose ends around their producing business, and then they said, "Talk to you later," and hung up.

Kip went to the tape machine and played the song again.

xi.

Mark shaved the beard he'd been absently growing. He looked happy and fit, like never before. "My work is done, Mom," he said. "The truck will be back tomorrow after-noon."

His departure turned out to be as sudden as his arrival. At least this time he cared to mention it during lunch. "Thanks for everything," he said.

"Too bad you're leaving," Josie said.

"Too bad?"

"I've gotten used to you around again."

"But you hardly saw me."

"I saw your bed, undone."

"Sorry."

"That's fine," Josie said. "I like the house better when it has that lived-in look. You found your soul, I take it."

"Yeah."

"What does it sound like?"

"I want you to know," Mark said, "for yourself."

He led her up to the attic, holding her hand up the tricky steps on the top floor.

Oh, boy, she thought. He was going to play her his grand masterpiece. She remembered all the times she had to focus on her enthusiasm for him and not the incomprehension he caused her. At least the pop songs she could dance to in an awkward sort of way. What sort of thing was waiting for her in the attic?

The attic was tidy, dryly ascetic. All the instruments were perched in their stands, all the wires hidden. Mark grabbed two bulky sets of headphones and handed one to her.

"Please sit down," he said, offering her a chair.

"Give it a spin," she said, putting on the headphones, hoping to at least tolerate it, hoping to come up with some specific comments, like that child-care book had suggested to her so long ago, in reference to the matter of giving encouragement to creative kids.

"I hope you like it," he said, and ran the tape.

The hum entered her ears and mesmerized her.

An empty room, the floorboards quivering underneath her feet. Her husband dying. The sound of bells tolling in slow motion, threatening to flutter below the threshold of her hearing. Realizing that she could not ever depend on him again, that he was not coming back. Shaking, scratching sounds, then a dull, solid throb, like pounding on pavement. The policeman's hands pulling open a plastic body bag to let her identify a car-crash victim who was thought to be her husband. A slowly rising wail, somewhere between a human voice and a violin, fuzzy and warm and expressive. The first time she let herself mourn him. The wail, growing stronger and more intensely sad. A feeling, all bunched up in her stomach and rising like heat out of her lungs and coming out in sobs, like hiccups. The wail rising up to the highest pitch and trailing off into echo. Releasing that heat with her breath and her voice and her tears, the feeling of having something pulled out from her. Whistles and whispers jumping left to right, as if they were thoughts inside her head. The wail, now more temperate, returning to envelop the image with more falling balls of glass. Another wail joining the first, a duet. Then three voices. Then four. Then five, and six, and seven, and so on, until an infinity of wailing noises joined one another, all saying the same thing, all calling for the same thing, all rising. All flooding in one another's warmth, in her own. Then the wails began trailing off until the one wail was left, wailing softly, in peace. The wail ended in a still, hopeful, even note and trailed off, leaving only a hum behind; a room now filled with love.

Josie took off the headphones.

"So," Mark said, "how did you like it?"

She now thought she understood her son. She longed for the same things, for love and security and peace, that he did. It was eerie to realize that what she wanted for him, and what he wanted for himself, and for others, was essentially the same. She could answer his question. Be specific, she thought. Be brave.

"Mark," she said, "do you know . . . when you're with someone and you feel they know you and you know them and your feelings are the same? When you kind of think you and that person aren't any different and that you understand them and you want the best for them and they want the best for you? You felt included by them and they included you?"

"Yes," he said, his eyes shining at her.

"Well," she said. "I never thought I could feel like that with most people."

"Neither did I."

"And I can feel it now, that warmth rising up on me."

"Me too."

"I never thought I could feel like that for you."

"I didn't either," Mark said, "until now."

"And I know you know, Mark," she said. "I know. It's a girl. You hurt for a girl. That's why you're hurt, and what you're lonely for. It's a girl."

"It's not a girl, Mom."

"Then, what is it?"

"It's a guy, Mom," Mark said. "It's a guy."

The news of this love could have disappointed her, but it didn't. Part of Josie just wasn't that surprised. But it still upset her to hear it.

"I thought you'd figured it out," Mark said. "I'm sorry."

Mark turned to the tape machine and set it on rewind.

"Maybe I just wasn't listening," Josie said.

"You have to want to hear it. You have to want to hear. It took me a long time to hear it, too. It took me a long time."

Josie pointed to the tape machine.

"Play it again," she said.

Index Card, Index Finger

i.

Dear Mary:

Before I forget, Mark sends his love.

Lately I've been quietly enjoying myself. It's like rolling forward toward the end of a book. You know there are few pages left and you read breathlessly to the end for its comforting feeling of closure. Soon I will lose my mind, and I'm looking forward to it.

That certainty comforts me. Everything about my disease has been laid out before me, and I know that it will happen. It's just a matter of when.

One of the things about knowing the end is nigh is how you can put all your energies into having your nigh end be as satisfying as possible. It took me all these years to get to that point. There are so many things I've been attached to—photographs, rare vinyl albums, suchlike—memorabilia, if you will. And I've been attached to so many things I've kept to myself and shared with no one. And now part of the fun is to give them away. You can imagine the look on Kip's face when I gave him my Velvet Underground collection. I wish I'd found some way to preserve that for posterity—lust and gratitude mingling in his face as he peeled the banana off the album cover. I never dared to do that myself and alter its collector's value. But I now delighted in seeing him do just that.

I've collected this vast amount of stuff, and it took me until now to know why.

Remember Cornell? Remember that I used to go through professors' trash cans to find dittos of their tests, incriminating love letters (and I found some really stupid ones), credit slips, phone bills, etcetera? I hope you do. I gave you all of my best stuff.

But not the best. . . . The best I kept to myself, and I never told you.

Remember that smug and cranky professor (whatsisname whatsisomething) who burned all his papers, his piles of index cards, in a little bonfire in his backyard? It was impossible to find anything from him, other than little tins of caviar.

Well, once I did find something.

I kept it to myself. Here I had a bit of someone else's junk, an index card with a few lines, thrown away. I rescued it and made it mine to keep close to my selfish, manly bosom.

You don't know the sick glee it gave me, hiding that from you. You don't know how much anguish it caused me as well. For part of me was dying to show it to you. But I thought you would love it, and if you did, it would no longer belong to me. It would be also in your head, like some little germ of thought, in your consciousness. And I wanted it only to be in mine.

It's like loving a record so much you really don't want it to hit the big time and have to enjoy it along with People Less Aesthetically Developed Than You.

And if you didn't love it, even like it—well, it

would have lessened me. I did not want to appear naïve, or shallow, or flaky.

Too late for that now!

I mean, if there was anything I kept from you—and there was not a lot—you were the first to know I lusted mightily in my heart for forbidden fruits (!), the first to know about my condition (did I ever tell you that you were the first? I think not). Well, this little fucking card had grown to Great Wall of China proportions, the more I revealed myself to you, as time went by—and believe me, when I didn't answer your cryptic, playful postcards and refused to look at your gift of a bluish butterfly, framed and suitable for hanging in that wall space in my kitchen—well, let's say that this card sort of made me unable to enjoy them and respond with the kindness they deserved.

No longer.

I wish to see the end of my days free from my junk, and to make that junk a symbol of my bonds, my junk bonds.

Pardon my terrible puns.

Herein the card, now yours, for you only.

Waiting for the world to end,

Dean.

ii.

A yellowed, creased index card was enclosed with Dean's letter. It read:

Do I mean a butterfly to be in a wooden box, with a pin struck through it? Should I mean to open a window, for it to fly through?

iii.

Mary opened a window in her office, and a wind blew through it, scattering the index cards, which she had carefully laid out on her desk to order the sequence of comedy bits for the coming weeks. The bit about pretending you're stupid in order to get better service when shopping fell on Thursday's row. The bit about having the hair on your ears trimmed at a posh haircuttery fell on Friday's. The bit about calling up famous people to find out which they liked best, chocolate or vanilla, fell on the floor. She'd forgotten where she'd decided to schedule the ice-cream census.

Such is the fate of the head writer. All of the work becomes about which night is best to schedule weaker or stronger premises—all depending on the guests, the night that would get the most audience, and the mood of the host. Of course, she came up with her share of jokes, but now most of her work was an act of critically balancing relative virtues, a Showbiz-Valu-Senso-Meter.

She refused to tack the things up on the cork board on her wall, and then untack and tack them as she made order of them. She wanted her pieces movable on a table top to do Comedy Stratego.

And so that Fifth Avenue wind, *El Monstruo,* shuffled her deck.

She decided it was time for lunch.

Lunch was one of those things Mary could count on being stable. She always ate at the same place, had the same dish for months at a time, read the papers, and went through her mail, if she received any. She had people write to her at work, where she could be more easily reached, and she could always get mail that she cared for, unleavened by junk mail, bills, and the word *Occupant.* On her way out of the office, she went to her mailbox and pulled out a letter which was clearly Dean's.

It was always a thrill to get a letter from Dean. Ever since they had spent summers apart in college, they had corresponded, going through periods of postal famine and plenty, but still, corresponding. They gave each other good phone, but that was still no substitute for a letter. After all, it was a dying art, and mad romantics that they were, they were suckers for it. And letters were where they told each other their most intense, important feelings. After all, she couldn't have just called up and said, "I'm thinking of getting a divorce," within earshot of the party of the other part. And on a page, the news of Dean being diagnosed with AIDS had seemed more gently told, although she could have killed the mailroom clerk.

As she waited for her salad to arrive, she opened the letter.

iv.

"Are you upset?" Dean asked her when she called him.

"No, not really," Mary said.

"Who are we kidding. Certainly not me, darling."

"I can't accept this," she said. "Why don't you send it to some library or something."

"Look, it's not like it's the Dead Sea Scrolls," Dean said. "Besides, I'm supremely indifferent, ahem, to what it would mean to others. I, however, care deeply about you, Alice, and I'd like you to consider what it would mean to you."

"Alice?"

"Just kidding," Dean said. "Just practicing for future reference. I am going to forget your name, you know."

"Dean, that's harder for me to take than you can imagine."

"I cannot imagine it. See? My mental faculties are already going."

"I don't know what to say . . ."

"Write me something, then," he said. "An index card will do for me, my dear."

V.

She pulled a bunch of index cards out of their shrinkwrap. She placed them flat in front of her on the kitchen table and wrote on them.

I wrote to Dean, from my parents' place, to New York, where he was spending his summer with friends. I missed him terribly and I wished I were with him.

One day we started to find sunsets boring.

I was relieved when he told me he was attracted to men. He was very nervous when he told me, trying not to hurt my feelings. But then he was upset that I hadn't taken it badly. Didn't he mean something to me? Sure. But I'd blamed myself for his lack of attraction to me. It wasn't my fault. Afterwards, when we held each other, there no longer was a lingering tension.

I was his covert girlfriend at a family gathering. I was so excited by the ruse I tried to neck with him in the porch to keep the joke going, and we fell off the rail, laughing.

He asked me if he could be my bridesmaid.

Mom and Dad were horribly disappointed by the fact that Dean was genetically indisposed to marrying me.

He said, after failing to make love to me, "I hope it was as good for you as it was for me."

I wondered, after I divorced, what it would have been like if Dean had been straight.

Shit, this is hard.

With his index finger on my lips, he kept me from complaining about him not liking the butterfly I gave him as a gift. His look was so sad, so unlike him, I decided to let it slide.

Mark said it was beautiful, and hung it on the wall to Dean's silence.

His index finger, succinct, thick-set, typetype-typing finger.

I collect my thoughts, I collect my memories. I think of ways of arranging them. I try to make them mean something, mean the most they can.

The index card. In context, a question of every-thing. By itself, just sentences on a piece of card-board.

That butterfly I gave Dean, I liked its blue phos-phorescence, and I knew Dean would like that too—the effect, and the word that goes with it.

If you'd looked at it closely, you'd have seen all the tones that made the texture a whole, all the dif-ferent shades.

To be honest, I can no longer remember exactly how that butterfly looked. It might have been pur-ple blue, green blue. I don't know if I should care or not. I might have made up that bit about the shades.

I can't remember. It's like I have to force it to be sentimental or it's not real.

Dean began a letter by saying he'd finally accepted having a dead bug on his wall. And he said, later on, that he was dying.

He said events had a nice simultaneity to them. I didn't know exactly what he meant.

Retrospectives.
Collector's items.
Collected stories.
Quilts, mosaics.
Wooden boxes.

Do I capture precisely what things mean?

Should I let things mean whatever they mean?

An index card.
An index finger.
A butterfly.
An open window.

vi.

Dear Mary:

I don't expect you to find me as interesting a letter writer as Dean, but he refuses to let me take dictation.

To be honest, he can't dictate too well at this point.

He loves to play with the Rolodex. He takes the cards out and puts them back in. In no order. He takes one and stares at it for a while. I've kept him from writing on them. Sometimes he takes them all out and drops them all over his bed with whatever energy he's got. Throws them away as if he were throwing them at some invisible hat on the corner of his bed.

He puts them back on the Rolodex, slowly. You can't imagine how many hours he whiles away on that. I don't think he even knows what they are about anymore, but don't take it badly. When he could, he did.

You can come visit anytime. I know it may be a shock for you. I can let you know what to expect. And then—you know him—he might surprise us.

Love,
Mark.

vii.

Mary held Dean, pinned against the hospital bed.
Dean put his index finger on her lips when she held him.
There was no lingering tension.

A Small Indulgence

All was well in the Afterlife until Mrs. Thelman's youngest son, Derek, who was still alive, made an appearance in the cupboard right before teatime.

Mrs. Thelman, Sarah to those she did not wish to keep at a distance, had been dead for twenty years by the time she looked for another bag of sugar and found Derek instead. She and Mr. Albert Thelman dwelt in a nice Victorian three-story-and-garden house in an area of Anglican Heaven not terribly close to the City of Light—as well it should be, they thought, given their mild natures, not too given to all manner of singing, whooping, bell clanging, and other heavenly celebrations. Their activities consisted of nice-novel reading, living-room lounging, and garden puttering. They would have, on occasion, dead people over for canasta, or would visit friends or long-dead family members they had not had the opportunity of looking down on while living. Sometimes they waited at the Pearly Gates for the Incoming, whom they had a duty to welcome by virtue of relationship, some of whom they never heard from again.

No, they did not wish to embrace most of the choices their status accorded them. They did not wish to look into the Living's lives from their cloudy perch; they did not wish to visit earthly planes and shake chains or noisy things around in people's attics. They chose not to take another lifetime, not to go to Heavenly Choir tryouts, not to change their faces or social status. This was their peaceful repose—

a stable, quiet life without risks or surprises, looking forward to nothing but the next pot of tea, spot on time.

On the afternoon of the uninvited appearance of their
son, Cousin John dropped by with a tin of biscuits. John
was an entertaining if slightly unseemly relation to whom
they owed thanks due to his role in the family history, circa
1921, when he charmed the couple's respective parents
into accepting their then recently uncovered courtship.
John had taken full advantage of Heaven's spoils. He'd
had another lifetime between visits, tooted horns with the
angels, traded shape and gender and genus at his whim.
Somehow they found his folly a matter for amusement and
even envy, and they were not genuinely displeased with his
shifting until he dropped by for tea as a gnu. And he always had news from the world outside their home.

This time, as a vaguely Persian prince of a man, John lit
Mr. Thelman's cigar in the smoking room with a fiery
sword.

"It's been bandied about," John said, "that Earth's current economic boom is soon to end. Lots of people going
broke—I'm sure it'll be fabulous watching. One gets bored
watching the basic tedium of the flesh life. . . ."

"What year is it now?" Thelman asked.

"Oh, I don't know, somewhere around the turn of the
century. In any case, the pub's running a gambling pool."

"I can't see why anyone would spend so much time
looking at people's lives like that," Thelman said.

"It's just something to do," John said.

"I find it altogether unpleasant," Mr. Thelman said. "If I
were alive, I would not like to have my privacy intruded on
by nosy ghosts."

"You sure didn't know it then, though."

"Beg your pardon?"

"Nothing, nothing," John said. "Look, you go to the
pub, you drink, you celebrate your well-earned rest by re-

minding yourself of how miserable and pathetic most people's lifetimes are. Besides, there's much more to do at the Wing & Halo."

"Like what?"

"Darts, Albert," John said in a tone of voice like eyes rolled in resignation.

Sarah appeared through the smoking room's doorway with the tea cart. Thelman and John noticed that there was no sugar bowl on the cart and that the teapot was missing its multicolor tea cosy.

Something was terribly amiss.

"Are you well?" Thelman asked.

"Oh, yes, yes I am," she said. "Just a bit under the weather."

"Darling," John said, "you look as if you've seen a . . . well, you don't look too well."

Mr. Thelman grabbed her hand. "You just sit down and I'll get the sugar—"

"No, don't fret, dear," she said. "I'll just go right back and fetch it—"

"No, no, you sit down and I'll get the sugar."

Thelman found the sugar bowl on the countertop with only a few shallow spoonfuls' worth in the bottom. He opened the dry-goods cupboard to find, between bottles of spice, his son's head.

"Hello, Father," his son said.

"Derek," Thelman said. He was more surprised that he'd used that name than at seeing Derek's head in such an inappropriate place. But Thelman wouldn't stand to think of this for too long. He grabbed the bag of sugar and closed the cupboard. He refilled the bowl. He opened the cupboard. Derek was still there.

"May I have a moment with you?" asked Derek.

"I'm afraid I can't speak with you," Thelman said.

"What, should I write?"

"You could have paid a call to your mother first."

"I did see her," Derek said. "But she wouldn't speak to me."

A light breeze came through the window, rustling the curtains, filling the space between words.

Thelman did not know how to address his son further. Thelman was a man whose social skills were, in moments of unease, limited to understanding bank statements. It did not help that he did not wish to speak to Derek. It had been so long since he'd spoken to him, even before he'd died. He didn't know why he'd even looked him in the eye, just then. He'd refused to set sight on that face. And yet, he was surprised by his son's countenance—jowly, white-haired, bespectacled respectability—and was surprised that he wanted to keep looking.

"Your mother looks awfully upset," Thelman said. "You shouldn't just pop in on her like that."

"I didn't mean to. . . . It's the best I could do. . . . You see, I'm not dead yet."

Thelman turned his eyes away and felt his resolve to stay silent in the face of disquiet. Derek was shunned as far as he'd been concerned, and that would not substantially change.

"Please leave my house," Thelman said.

Thelman hated to see people begging for attention.

And he would not have Derek speak to him.

"All right, Father," Derek said.

And with that, Derek vanished, leaving behind a smell of rusty pennies and thwarted intentions.

Thelman put the lid on the bowl and carried it to the smoking room, pacing his breath.

"You must tell me what happened," John said, taking his cousin's hand.

"I do not want to bother you with the details," Sarah

said. "It must have been just some momentary lapse of mind—are they supposed to happen? I thought these kind of things would be over, now that we've made our place in Heaven. . . ."

"I'm afraid they don't," John said. "Unless you want them to. This . . . thing you're referring to—"

Sarah had a habit of looking down at the floor when someone spoke to her about matters she was not willing to contemplate. This had helped her observe with intense acuity sections of carpet, corners of tile, and cracks in linoleum during the expanse of her life. The cigarette burn on the brown and burgundy garland-patterned carpet, which they hadn't bothered to will out of existence, became her item of study.

"I'm afraid that the matter is closed," she said.

"It is not curiosity, but concern that drives me to beg you to let me hear you out," John said.

"No, I am well," she said, "Let's just drop the subject."

The burnt circle on the carpet . . . she hoped it would loom large like a pit and swallow her. She feared this moment as she had feared walking through old houses as a young child, as she had feared seeing things others would not believe: ghosts, fairies, angelic visitations. Maybe she should just get a new carpet after all. . . .

"All right," John said. "If you're not going to bother to give me a shred of your attention, I might as well not bother to be kind."

"I do not mean to decline your kindness," Sarah said. "I just don't think it a proper subject for discussion."

"What, you found a corpse in the cupboard?" John said. "Like it could happen here."

"Precisely," she said, and she poured tea for three, avoiding the thought of how much Derek spoke like her cousin.

Her husband entered the scene, bowl in hand.

"I see you all started without me," he said in his usual even tone of voice.

"Thank you, dear," she said, her calm restored by her husband's apparent obliviousness to the apparition. "I just knew you wouldn't be long, and I wanted the tea to be ready for you. Sorry to be so distracted."

"Not at all, darling," Thelman said. "It's bound to happen. You should get some rest."

"I'm sorry to spoil it for you," John said, "but you are dead. This *is* your rest."

"Because we are in it doesn't mean we have to overstate it," John said.

Sarah poured sugar into the cups. Thelman put some cream in his. John stared at them, watched them having tea in silence, all the while unable to feel scorn for them.

John was surprised when Sarah called him up to give her a ride to the City of Light. She rarely crossed over to the other side of the hedges, much less left her neighborhood. He suspected that Sarah, as usual, was counting on him to baby-sit her through some situation. John drove his MG up the Thelman's driveway and honked his horn.

Sarah walked out the door. Her black dress and hat seemed to John a mite too sensible. Sarah at first didn't recognize him. John smiled quietly until it registered that this elderly Chinese woman in the red MG was her cousin.

"Oh, John," she said, and slipped into the car.

"I just wanted to seem wise and inscrutable for a change," John said by way of an explanation, and started off to the highway. "So where do you want me to take you?"

"I understand that the Bureau of Information is somewhere in the City Center."

John noted she wasn't precisely comfortable with the trip. "What?" he said. "Looking for some useful information?"

"Nothing special," she said. "I was thinking of looking up Maude's Incoming date so as to have a nice dinner party in her honor. You know her, she was so kind to us during the war. . . ."

"Oh, I remember, Maude Akins? Last I heard she was blubbering away at a nursing home."

"Must you be so vulgar?"

"Yes, I must."

They drove toward the hazy outlines of bright, shiny gold and glass domes and boxes in the distance. Traffic got tighter as the City of Light loomed closer. An on-ramp from the Mormon subdivision spilled into the road, and John and Sarah found themselves in Joseph Smith-lock.

"Traffic jams are forever," John said.

Albert Thelman hoed his own personal piece of paradise, keeping up his hobby of award-winning flower gardening, working on beds of jack-in-the-pulpit, love-lies-bleeding, Dutchman's breeches, and phlox. He was turning over a new bed to plant some less exotically named vegetation. An interruption came in the shape of a well-shod foot in the way of his swiftly swung hoe.

"Ow!" Derek shouted, rising up from the sod, and he hopped about a bit, shaking off dust and pain. "That was rather painful, Father."

Father went on turning soil, minding the worms he'd raised from the underground, careful to ignore Derek completely. He stood to wipe his brow with a handkerchief and looked at the sky.

"Father?" Derek said. "It's me. Derek."

The sky was clear, with only a few clouds and a few low-flying seraphim and cherubim floating in the glassy sea of Heaven.

"You cannot possibly imagine how hard it has been for

me to concentrate and think of you as a presence in my mind," Derek said. "It seems so phony to me."

Mr. Thelman put down his instrument and took a step toward the house.

"Father," Derek said, "can you give me your attention?"

Mr. Thelman walked steadily to the back door. For a moment he felt the impulse to stop. To turn back. But he wouldn't go back on his word.

"I know we haven't spoken for a long time," Derek said. "But, after all, I'm only visualizing you. . . ."

Thelman opened the back door and closed it behind him.

Derek let a short, slim breath leave through his nose and opened his eyes. He couldn't even imagine his own father speaking to him.

A small consolation to Sarah and John was the ready availability of parking space near the Bureau of Information. They entered the tastefully appointed lobby and Sarah shyly asked the information booth the whereabouts of Incoming Services.

Sarah started to feel some apprehension at her deceit, which always tinged her resolve with timorousness. Her husband did not know where she was. Her cousin thought she was looking for someone else's Incoming date. She was not accustomed to lying—just to withholding certain things. All to cover for her curiosity. . . .

"I hope this does not take too long," she said as she entered the elevator. "I must be home for dinner."

"Don't worry," her cousin said, "we're still on schedule." Not that there really was any need for one.

The Incoming Reference Library was a vision in dark wood and bronze fixtures. People floated up and down the tall walls, pulling out folders, floating down to inspect them at leisure on quaint desks with wells where ink bottles used to sit.

John enjoyed watching Sarah glow in awe and blush with confusion. It drew him back to their youth and led him to believe that she had not completely turned into a stable, well-pleased middle-class wife. It made her annoying dependency on his complicity feel like trust.

"Just think of the filing," John said. "I understand that if you go to the desk at the far corner of the room you can ask for help. Or I can do it for you, if you wish."

"Thank you, but no," she said. John heard her struggling not to be curt. "I would rather inspect them on my own."

John looked at her thin-lipped composure. "Very well," John said. "I shall be out on the street. I trust you can find me."

He turned to the elevator. He was accustomed to letting Sarah determine just how much he intruded on her existence. This was not the first time she had excluded him, and it wouldn't be the last. Strange how he would defer to her, as if she held some power over him; strange how he would allow her not to let him in. As if he didn't deserve her trust. In other situations, he could exhort, negotiate, persuade, seduce, charm, and draw people into his confidence. Not as a power play, but as a measure of his desire to be, to put it simply, close to them. He could not stand to be separate from others. He lived for closeness, for involvement. For no other reason, he was an attaché from the Celestial Interborough Agency, envoy to the suburbs of Heaven. For nothing but this, he was known as a valued member of the celestial community and of the intelligence community. But, hands off Sarah, when she said so.

He thought she could be unnecessarily secretive about the most unimportant things. He guessed even close relations would need to keep something to themselves, but . . .

well, he was not going to turn back and ask her to satisfy
his curiosity. It would be too much to ask.

"Derek Thelman?" the clerk said, looking through a catalog of the Existing.

"Yes," Sarah said. "Perhaps you can fetch me his file?"

"Sure." The clerk floated up like a spaceman through
the vacuum of space and reached a shelf-level way too high
for Sarah to follow with her eyesight. He dropped back
down and handed her a thick envelope tied with string.

"You may look through it to your heart's content," he
said, smiling broadly.

"Thank you kindly," she said. She carried the heavy
file—so long a life, she thought—toward a desk, and sat
down to peruse it.

She did not care to read the file so much as to confirm
the status of her son. She skipped through the documen-
tation from his guardian angel—it wasn't up to date, only
covering until last week. She reached the most recent
entry—a prayer he had posted up to Heaven.

Yes, he was still alive.

The news that her son was, after all, not dead, was,
strangely, good news. She had not spoken to him for many
years, since he . . . since he did what Mr. Thelman had
shielded her from knowing. But it was good news that he
was alive.

There were, the records said, about twenty more years
to go before Derek would kick the bucket.

How could have he gotten through to her? What did he
want? What could she do to keep him from speaking to his
father? It would upset Mr. Thelman, and she would have
to bear seeing him bitter and curt and quiet for many a
day. He would make her pay for her son's imprudence.
And she did not wish to be stuck in the Afterlife with the
same thing she was stuck with in life. No. She would not

pursue the matter further. She resolved to avoid seeing her son, or thinking about him.

"I'm ready to go," Sarah said, walking up to the bench where John sat cross-legged, pensively.

John looked up at her. "Oh, I'm sorry," John said. "I was thinking of something."

"Shall we go?"

"We shall, Your Majesty, the bloody Queen."

Now, where did that come from? Sarah asked herself.

John was leaving the Thelmans' house, about to step into the MG, when he was assaulted by Derek, the apparition.

"Um . . . are you a friend of the family?" Derek asked.

"Derek!" John said. "Old chap, I'd hope to hear about your demise so as to welcome you to this next world, but, let me welcome you now, nonetheless—"

"Who the hell are you and how do you know my name?"

John had forgotten that he was in the shape of an elderly Chinese woman.

"Oh, I'm sorry," John said, "give me a second to change."

The hunched back straightened, shoulders spread, breasts turned to muscles, arms and legs grew long and lanky and hairy, the short, black, straight hair flowed over his ears, turned wavy light brown with blond highlights, the forehead stretched back to meet a receding hairline, the thick lips became thinner, less pouty, until he practically had no lips, the round jaw turned square, dark brown eyes turned cornflower blue. With fewer lines than he had the last time he lived in flesh, he was state-of-the-art mid-thirties John Abbadon Raithe in a dandifying dark gray piped velour jacket and a wide red silk neck accessory tied up in a thick, flowery bow. It was anachronistic—he had been a glint in his father's eyes in the age of absinthe—but it suited him.

"John!"

"Right you are." John went to slap his unofficial nephew. His hand went through him.

"I'm not quite the ghost yet," Derek said.

"You're not?" John said. "How charming. May I ask how you've accomplished this?"

"Well," Derek said, "I'm not really here, this is just my visualization. You see, I'm imagining that I'm having this conversation with you so as to deal with unresolved feelings that haunt me. You, in a sense, are just a figment of my dramatization."

"If I didn't know you well I'd be insulted," John said. "But no, I'm afraid I'm a very real experience to myself."

"I'd imagine you'd say that," Derek said.

"No matter," John said. "What can I do for you."

"I want you to ask Mother and Father to speak to me."

"Why don't you ask them that yourself? After all the trouble you've gone to to be here—"

"I have," Derek said. "They won't acknowledge my presence. I'm invisible to them. I begged and pleaded with Mother for a response right to her face."

"Was she looking at the floor?"

"Yes."

"I see."

"Father's no good either. But him not wanting to see me, at first, I can understand."

"How so?"

"I'm afraid that's a personal matter."

"I guess I'm not meant to know, heh?" John said.

"Look, it's nothing personal, and it's nothing I'm terribly proud of."

"Very well," John said, "but I'm afraid that your mum and dad don't consider me the voice of reason, not to mention compassion."

"I beg you to speak to them," Derek said. "Intercede on

my behalf. I really wish to speak with them. I am too old to carry old grudges. . . . Indulge me, please. I know that Elysian Fields are not for the living to visit, but I must speak with them."

"I'm afraid that's beyond my reach," John said. "Your mother and father, to be honest, don't keep me in their confidence, and they don't listen to me unless it's a function of how useful I am to them. My situation is compromised."

"But can't you do this for me?" Derek said. "Can't you just ask them for me? It won't take anything, not so much as a blink of an eye."

"The dead don't blink," John said.

Derek looked exhausted. It evidently took a lot out of him to be here. All of his energy, all of his faith. John felt terrible that Derek had wasted his time.

"I just want to tell you," Derek said, "when you died, I always thought you watched over me. That you could see everything I did and thought and felt clearly. And that somehow terrified me, and thrilled me. It made me feel loved."

"I did," John said, smiling, slightly embarrassed. "That I did."

Derek could be so charming. . . .

"What is it that you want to know?" John said. "Why must you speak with them?"

"I just want to know if they're happy. I wouldn't know how to ask them."

"This is Heaven, you know."

"Are they happy?" Derek asked.

"Of course they are," John said. "As you know, they live what they consider to be a happy . . ."

Something flickered inside John.

No, they were bloody not happy. He knew he was lying.

Derek looked at him, so much hope in his eyes.

". . . They like their house, and they enjoy their stability."

"Are you happy?"

Funny how nobody ever bothered to ask him that question.

The sky . . .

"I don't know," John said.

The sky above . . .

"Some kind of Heaven this is, then," Derek said.

The sky above them turned to dusk.

"I don't know," John said. "I don't really know what this is, sometimes."

They stared at each other.

Derek soon disappeared, and night fell after.

A few months later, Sarah and Albert wondered why John hadn't paid them a call at teatime, or at all. They passed the sugar to each other, quietly.

§

Quintessence

It was Friday, five o'clock, frenzied: rarely did these items occur with such simultaneity. Friday evenings were (mostly) nothing all that special: a night to go shopping for rare record albums in the Village, to watch the odd art film, or to browse through used-bookstore shelves, alone. Dean seldom rushed out of his office, briefcase in tow, pulling hat over head, a fire under his butt. Nor would he have a reason to, stopping only to ceremoniously twiddle with his bow tie and readjust his gray tweed and tawed elbow-patch jacket and check his chained vest-pocket watch. But tonight: he's late, he's late, yet, O, he lifted his hat and inspected the shininess of his extended forehead. A cruel, figurative cow had grazed and razed the once wavy black landscape of his scalp, and now that hair was merely a memory, now his head was a bare and shapely field, a milky-pink pate, a blank space, with no sign of cow or landscape, signifying nothing. The happy few hairs left to Dean, about three at last count, were shaved off every week in the interest of maintaining a sort of dignified consistency in the face of this terrible loss. And his bald dome of thought lacked luster, thank God. Would he light his pipe or not? *Ceci n'est pas une pipe,* he muttered, under his breath, slipping the smoking implement into a pocket. Translation (mundane usage, French colloquial): This is not a pipe, this is not a blow job. A mere image of what may be, analysis would reveal. Sometimes a pipe is not a pipe. It's an *illuuu-zhon, mon frère,* he told himself, applying some fun to that obscure object of his folly. For he was about to go out on a date—a first date!—with someone who, a few days ago, was a complete nobody other than as a small collection of specifics: worked downstairs, nice person, hubba hubba. Now he knew him a bit better: gay, available, interested. Now he would know him a lot better.

Whee!

ii.

"Bob!" Dean said. "I mean, Bob. . . . I hope I didn't make you wait too long."

"That's all right," Bob said. "I know you get off work an hour later than me. I've gotta be here earlier. All the packages come in so early in the morning."

"Still, you didn't need to wait so long for me. You could have met me at the restaurant."

"I don't know . . . it's not the same," Bob said. "I wanted it to be kinda special, so I waited so we could leave together."

"If you say so. . . ." Are you trying to flatter me in some inarticulate way? he thought. It's working.

"Let's go, big guy." Bob pressed the shoulder of his date, who stood about a foot lower than him. The term *big guy* and the gesture meant to Dean a warm acceptance of his relative smallness and reassurance that he hadn't totally ruined the evening. *You're a big guy, nothing to worry about—I will be the love of your life!* —Silly rabbit, Dean thought, turning, in the smithy of his self, one quality into another, a constant, playful re-invention of the meanings that presented themselves to him, like water into wine into blood into lemons into lemonade, none more substantial than the other.

"I hope this place is not too expensive," Bob said, as they approached the restaurant. "I'm kind of a starving artist. . . ."

"I prefer to eat at starving-artist prices," Dean said, "and I'm in the mood for guy food. Nothing fancy."

"Good," Bob said quietly. "I would hate not to know how to eat something."

A twinkle of affection gleaned off Dean's subtle atomies.

"Tonight I'm eating with my hands," Dean said.

They entered the fun-food-for-young-people restaurant and waited for the front-desk person to call their reservation into being—apparently the table promised to the two had failed to be substantiated in time, and they were stuck waiting with a big crowd of people in the teeny anteroom. In this interim between one state and another, in this uncertainty of things in process (shall my molecules go liquid or straight into steam?), small talk had to be made.

"How was work today?" Dean said, standing on the tips of his toes, speaking over the din of the restaurant into Bob's ear, Bob leaning down to listen.

"All right," Bob said. "Nothing special." He shrugged. He looked so deeply into Dean's eyes that he seemed about to kiss him, so close together were they in the purgatorial wait-to-be-seated area. "So, you must meet a lot of interesting people, upstairs. It must be really interesting."

Sexual tension, party of two, your table is ready.

"*My,*" Dean flamed, grabbing Bob's hand, then extravagantly manicuring his nails with an imaginary nail file. "I'll bet you *mahn*-sters lead such *inn*-teresting lives. . . . I said to my girlfriend just the other day, 'Gee, I bet *mahn*-sters are *inn*-teresting,' I said . . ."

This was Dean's secret Camp test: if effective, it revealed whether the person tested had a problem with effeminacy (yours, his, anybody's), especially in public. Dean didn't want to associate with anyone who'd ask him to suppress his quintessentially Camp instinct ("Can't you talk like a man?" "It's embarrassing when you throw your scarf around your neck with a flourish" "You are too glib/ smug/blasé/flaming"). Besides, it was his way of releasing the tension of determined interpretations: he couldn't live without its sweet transgression.

". . . The places you must go and the things you must see—*mm-yyy* stars. . . !" Dean added.

Bob loved it. Bob loved it so much he found it knee-slapping, doubling-over hysterical. A belly laugh wasn't the effect Dean had intended. Is he stoned? Dean thought. It wasn't *that* funny. It was just meant to break the ice.

"Man!" Bob said. "You do a great Bugs Bunny!"

"*Thank* yew!" Dean said, even more surprised (and thankful!) that Bob got his allusion (in-joke), and, finally, relieved that the jest didn't blow up in Bob's face and frighten and anger him, like a big orange monster.

But still, it wasn't that funny.

"Now let's dip our patties in the water," Dean said, still holding Bob's big fingers, cracked dry by hard labor, in his tiny, paw-like hands.

iii.

Dean came to the conclusion that Bob was not a rocket scientist. Bob took his time reading the menu with a concentration that disturbed our hero's sense of certainty. But that meant nothing, didn't it? Dean thought. There had to be more to Bob than his reading ability, social skills, conversational style. There had to be more to him than his body, his features, as singularly well-built and clean-cut as he was in his orange wool workshirt, jeans, and canvas high-tops. There had to be some kind of soul to him, and he thought souls were what he fell in love with, but what could reveal that to him, in the event deep conversation failed to happen, other than some kind of metaphysical x-ray vision?

Dinner conversation began with them talking shop— the people they worked with at the auction house, how the system could be improved—from the particular perspectives of their respective offices. Nothing new there. Then, in reference to Dean's question about his hobbies, Bob called himself an artist for the second time.

"The whole thing is," Bob said, "to add a certain, I don't know . . . a certain thing to it. Like it's not just a doily, or a candle, or a toilet-paper cosy. It's like it's art. You know?"

"I think I do," Dean said. "Like alchemy."

"Yeah, like magic, right? You'll see what I mean when you come up to my apartment," Bob said matter-of-factly.

Dean was bemused, if a bit threatened, by the obvious quality of the pass. It was one thing to openly acknowledge your intentions; it was another to make it so blatant, so lacking in romance, *nuance*. Dean felt it sort of took away from the swoon of the moment when it would finally happen, the moment where it was all clear and unavoidable and he just dived into it, damn all. . . . Without that sublime quality, it wasn't the same.

Dean was above casual sex. Maybe it had nothing to say to him, like a badly rendered simulation of a veined, varicolored wooden surface. The kind of thing that doesn't pretend to grander things, or cast an illusion. Translation: When sex was just sex, with no pretentions of being anything other than what it was at the precise moment of its occurring (no stretching back to the past to inform the events leading up to it with a salacious prefiguring of its actuality, no penetration into the future, transforming its vague existence into a purposeful event-to-come, a shape that was coming into focus, leaping and bounding toward him, the open arms of a loved one, waiting at the end of the tunnel, saying "welcome, my love, welcome" as one moved

toward it, inexorably) . . . when sex was just sex, it didn't
mean a thing to him. He didn't even like it, it was like a religious obligation of some kind to have sex with strangers
just to express his testosterone. Maybe, Dean thought, he
was a snob.

So Bob had just practically killed his chances of having
sex with him. His pass had no timing, no class. But he
might as well let it slip. He'd been far too much of a fuss-
budget regarding dates for the last few years, and they had
the frequency of blue moons.

Accept all invitations was his new motto.

Bob was one of the guys at receiving, where all the
knicknacks and collectibles (porcelain bovines, animation
cels) were unpacked and then delivered upstairs to him.
Bob had caught him reading *Christopher Street,* pipe
ablaze, in the little room the staff used to eat and smoke in.
Far from beating him up at the end of the day, Bob had
asked him for a date. Needless to say, Dean was relieved,
and more than a little excited. The effect that picking things
up and carrying them around had on Bob's physique was
not lost on Dean. And Bob was always nice to him, without
a hint of the attitude that receivers gave to the people who
catalogued the objects that they postaged or handled.

Bob was nice, and way bigger than him, and a little on
the slow side. But Dean was willing to see what came out
of their interactions, in spite of his already existing objections (OK, so maybe he was a looney tune, too). Maybe
Bob was painfully inarticulate, that was all, and painfully
inarticulate people, in his experience, often had the sweet-
est, most embarrassingly tender things to say.

"I have some etchings I'd like to show you, too," Dean
said.

"You etch?"

"No, it's just a turn of phrase."

Bob anxiously twirled the fork inside his baked potato.

"It's a *joke*," Dean said, "a *line*. Like 'baby, what's your sign?'"

"Oh, I get it, I thought you meant you were an artist, too."

"No, I don't make art."

"At least you know what it looks like," Bob said reassuringly.

Bob put his hand on Dean's knee (just so). The look of passion in Bob's face was so real, so sincere, the touch so almost not there, a ghostly hand upon his gray corduroyed kneecap. Dean felt a tingle, then a shiver between his shoulders, and an instant erection hardened against the texture of his ardor. He felt his head turn hot and red at the sudden intrusion of rapture. And Bob's face—rough with stubble, thick yet contoured of lip and nose and jaw, blue of eye, curly brown of hair—Bob's face dimpled, softly limned with warmth. He was rugged and handsome, always. He was extraordinarily lovable all of a sudden.

They went to Bob's apartment on the Lower East Side.

iv.

Dean looked at a candle in Bob's small, cramped bedside display of works, trying really hard not to wield his claws (me-*owrr!*). The candle had three colors—a black base, orange in the middle, and yellow on top. Candy corn with a fuse. The rest of the candles were of muddy, indefinite mixed shades, or in layered color combinations or swirls that neither Mother Nature's sense nor any art director's book ever pretended to match. The ones made with readymade molds were carelessly finished, sloppy and indelicate, with uneven seams that hadn't been sanded down, wobbly bases, and off-center wicks; the ones encased in tall glass, like votive candles, had air bubbles. The little dolls, with state colors and pageant banners sewn over their chests and roughly finished little dresses made with polyester or feathers or macraméd soft-colored twine, their arms extended to receive the fame that was coming to them while hiding toilet paper underneath their wide skirts . . . they were breathtakingly ugly in design and execution.

"I've sold all the doilys," Bob said. "But I'm going to stitch some up soon. You know, this stuff, it's saying something . . . on femininity and masculinity. Hopefully, I'll be able to get all my stuff into a gallery, where I feel it really belongs."

"Do you really think so?"

"Why do you ask?"

Ah, how could he say this politely? "You should work on your craft."

"I am working on it. I'm serious about that. But I care about it. I have something to say."

"What I mean is . . . what I mean is, if you work on your craft first, before you hit the galleries . . . you can focus on it, see it as it really is, and then practice it to perfection. . . . You know, give it a sense of value as a finished object . . . value in the *perfection* of it, beyond its intention. . . . You know, sincerity's not *enough*. . . . Maybe do some things you haven't tried before."

"Let me show you something new I just finished," Bob said. "I don't know if it's any good, so I didn't put it out for you to see. . . . I wanted you to find it."

Dean was so torn. Bob was so simple, so sweet, and he meant it to be artful. (It wasn't even craftful.) And it was all made from kits. The cognitive dissonance between intention and object seemed both pathetic and sad, naïve and profound; the objects themselves expressed nothing but a kind of hunger for recognition. The starving artist pulled his latest piece from underneath a pillow.

"It's a pillow, or a doll," Bob said, "or a pincushion, depending how you see it."

It was a blue moon. A fat, banana-shaped pillow the size of his palm, blue satiny cloth, awkwardly sewn and stuffed, with a little, felt sleeping cap, a sleepy felt eye, and a sleepy felt smile.

"I made it without a kit," Bob said, "on my own. You made me laugh so hard when I asked you out, and you said that you went on a date once in a blue moon. So I made it. For you. That's what it means."

It meant heartbreak. A banal image, rendered with a child's care for detail, was full of tender love for Dean, someone Bob hardly knew, someone who all this time was covertly condescending to him because he wasn't a rocket scientist. But the chemistry was there, that sexy charge between their intimate subtle atomies. But not the aesthetics. O God, he hated himself for being such a fucking snob, even as he stuffed the object into his jacket pocket as if he cared. Dean was so conflicted, so moved by the gesture, so repelled by the actual object, that he would have cried in fury had he not looked up to see Bob let his shirt fall on the floor.

Yipe!

Bob was beautiful, far more beautiful than the product of Dean's imagination, chest and arms and waist and shoulders that were designed by some perversely accurate architect (Oh, God comes to mind), sloping and bulging and spreading and contracting in the right places. And the hair on his arms and his chest and his sculpted belly seemed as if they had been copiously feathered on with a sensuous brush, not one hair in the wrong place.

And Bob held his arms out, and moved in on Dean, and held him oh so gently. And Dean leaned on his chest, thinking about what he had thought when he agreed to see him, and the conditions he accepted so naturally, when he should have been more cautious and set down rules and let himself know that this man, this beautiful man was not only *not* his intellectual equal but was probably slightly retarded. He was too simple to be intelligent, or maybe that was his prejudice talking, and he wanted to make love to him so badly, to enter him and transform him, in that tender place inside him, where maybe these things didn't count, didn't count at all. But that would be a great big fucking mistake, sex doesn't do that, penetration isn't liberation, not freedom of any sort, not release from the verities of the human heart, from the truth that he could not love (his biggest fear) someone he couldn't really understand, someone who couldn't really understand him. It was as if they spoke different languages. He couldn't imagine a future with him.

"Bob," Dean said.

"Yeah, baby?"

"I don't really think we should do this."

Bob slowly unlocked his arms from around Dean. He looked at Dean with a little smile that was confused more than frustrated.

"You think so?" he said.

"Bob . . . you and I are both artists. And, you know, you really can't have two artists in the same family."

"Says who?"

" I can't ask you to compromise your . . . artistic vision so I can have mine. If you and I don't work out . . . it would be really hard for us to work together. It would just be . . . confusing. And I would really hate to bring this into the office."

Bob's dimples lost their depth. He looked contrite before a scolding.

"You're a really sweet guy, and, God, you turn me on like crazy," Dean said. "But, you've got to consider, there's more at stake. If we end up hating each other, work would be hell. That's not to mention the unfortunate effect this could have on our private labors."

Bob let his face drop, clicked his lips, and stared away, lost, at some distant thought.

"Come on, sweetie," Dean said, lifting Bob's face up with a finger, trying to get into his eyes. "It's my mistake. I should have brought this up. I just got so carried away, you know, being asked out by you."

"Thank you," Bob said.

"And, who knows? If it had happened any other way, maybe we'd be boyfriends. With a house with a white picket fence, and everything."

"I want that, too," he said, raising his eyebrows plaintively. "That means a lot to me."

"And I want it so much, hon, I want it so much. But I can't responsibly see you and risk disaster. My work is too valuable to me . . . and I suppose your work means a lot to you too."

(Bob had lit one of the candles, a muddy purple one, when they came in.)

"I'd hate to lose my job," he said. "But I want to be in love."

"I hate to do this," Dean said, "but you've *got* to understand that this is for our art. . . ."

(The candle lit unevenly. It had taken Bob two tries to light it.)

"I understand," Bob said quietly.

(The muddy purple candle had gone out by this time.)

"Can I kiss you before you go?" Bob said.

Dean grabbed him. Dean kissed him with all his passion, and fury, and hope, and almost threw him over the display of handmade objects of love.

V.

As he stormed off westward, hat planted firmly on head and briefcase aswing, hoping to catch a taxi before a mugger caught him, Dean wondered if this looking for love was something he was unsuited for, if he was too much a man of the mind (or if he should be looking for love at NASA) —

· Now, *now* he really knew what a nasty little shit he was, how profoundly and sublimely stupid and small he was, and he dearly, dearly wished that their kiss had transformed, translated, transubstantiated him, somehow, but it hadn't—it had just pulled the rug from underneath his feet. He wished he could love without holding back, that he could purify his passion to its fifth essence, into an ecstasy that obliterates all sensibilities and judgments and accepts all and everything, into a magically charged object that could change his mean spirit into a soul of gold.

8
8

A Note on the Aesthetics and Ideology of Interesting Monsters

Let me take a moment to exalt the rightfulness of my product by framing my entire *oeuvre* as second fiddle to the tendentious urges of a theory. In the process of assiduously marginalizing other less-cool intellectual confections— otherwise, it wouldn't be widely disseminated as a cultural practice or market category—ReModernism provides for occasions such as essayistic interventions in fiction anthologies. A norm for questioning norms that makes my work look like the most questioning norm for norm-questioning, ReModernism is twice as effective as Modernism and gets there before PostModernism. It comes out in the encyclopedia next to Remodeling, so gay guys will stumble on it. As of this writing, the ReMo project seeks to appropriate and commandeer the human conversation in order to free itself. Bristling with ReModernity, *Interesting Monsters* thusly infiltrates, disembodies/dispirits, and cancels all norms and tendencies; without this justification, and distributable media such as a Graywolf Press publication, the poor thing would be illegitimate or illegible.

§

Ghosts, Pockets, Traces, Necessary Clouds

i.

From the kitchen, Mark heard the lock on his apartment door open with a sudden clunk. He turned a rubber band around four pieces of fan mail and put a kettle on the stove to boil. He heard the soft rustling of his lover's jacket as it settled on the coatstand by the door.

It had been a few weeks since he last saw Jules; he had felt him slipping out of his grasp the last time he saw him, when Mark gave him a key to his apartment. Jules had spent too much time talking about his wife. He said he really did not love her but he was inviolably married to her. Still, Mark tolerated Jules's attempt at drawing pity and comfort from him; that was a minor drawback. To listen and maybe counsel was a small price to pay for a fairly consistent, unobstrusive affair.

They both wanted a sex life without the hassles. Mark in particular didn't want to spend all his money looking for sex anymore, but he wouldn't have told that to Jules. And Mark didn't want to put Jules on the spot by asking for some promise of security. It would be too much trouble to renegotiate their friendship. Mark had chosen to put out the flags that said he wanted to be fucked, no strings attached, no romance involved, and he wouldn't change his tune now.

Maybe this would encourage Jules to spend more time

with him, after all: having Mark's apartment as a pocket of abandon in a universe of heavy burdens and responsibility. And it was up to Mark to keep things light. Hence: the unshod feet, the T-shirt too thin and shrunk to fold into shorts too tight for pockets, the ginseng tea in sweltering weather. And he would try the it's-too-hot-to-wear-a-suit, why-don't-you-put-on-some-shorts? gambit.

Jules was just right. Sweet or aggressive at just the right times, independent but not cold. Jules wore the suit but not the attitude. Mild in public, wild in private. Certainly not a fan boy: Mark's past fame meant nothing to him, if he even knew about it. Nor did he care for music. He was a regular guy who liked to have sex with men, Mark in particular. Just what Mark wanted, nobody militant, especially overtly so—a trustworthy man, straight-acting, for all the world innocent of secrets. That Jules liked to fall in love with men was something that wasn't an issue when they met late one night at a very expensive, selective bar on the Upper East Side. A place named Indiscretions, the kind of place that has no sign or front window, known only by word of mouth.

"Hi," Jules said. "Sorry I'm late."

"I'm starting to get accustomed to it," Mark said. "Would you like to take a seat? I'm making some tea."

"Thank you," Jules said, pulling out a chair from the breakfast nook. "Isn't it too hot for tea?"

"No time to brew and chill it. I could pour it over ice, if you like." Mark pulled down two mugs from the cupboard, conscious of how Jules was taking quick, interested glances at his legs, and chest, and privates. Mark almost stopped to pose for him to stare at, but that would be too funny. Just a casual tease, an obvious attempt to seize Jules's attention, a flirt that Mark wouldn't allow himself in public—being so obvious, demonstrative. Mark placed small tea strainers on the mouth of each mug. "But it's ginseng tea, it's meant to be hot," Mark added. He shook tea leaves from a tiny tin box into the strainers. "Wouldn't want to upset any Chinese gods."

Mark shot Jules a what-are-you-lookin'-at? eye, making Jules blush.

"Wouldn't want to do that," Jules said. Jules, fingering his tie loose under his collar, looked at the packet of letters. Mark felt urgently the need to take those letters away. He should have hidden them. And yet he couldn't stop Jules from undoing the rubber band.

"Fan letters," Mark said, coldly. "Pretty juvenile."

"You get fan mail? How come that doesn't surprise me?"

"Before we met, I was a recording artist."

"Before the small-home-repairs thing?"

"During," Mark said, sitting down, the water burbling in the kettle. "It's interesting how some people write to you, still."

"You, a musician?" Jules said. "Why didn't you tell me?"

"It's just something I did."

Jules began to unfold the flap of a beige envelope, addressed in purple ink. "Can I look?"

Mark quickly took the other letters from the table, and tapped the tabletop with the hard paper edge of the envelopes. Jules stopped short of pulling out a page or two of typed, sticky erasable bond.

"I prefer you don't," Mark said softly.

"I'm just curious," Jules said, "I don't mean to intrude."

Mark stood up to take the whistling teapot off the flame.

"Well, it isn't like I'm going to take over your life," Jules said.

"It isn't," Mark said. Mark brought over the mugs.

"It's not like I don't have a key to your place," Jules said.

"It's a privilege I give to few."

Jules chuckled as Mark poured tea. "Mark, you can be

so fuckin' imperious! If I've 'earned' your trust enough to let me in anytime I want to come in, you could at least feel comfortable."

Mark dipped the strainer in and out of the steaming cup with a slight shake of his wrist. "Would you want me to drop by your house?"

"No," Jules said. "Certainly that's not what we've agreed to."

"So don't read my mail," Mark said, removing the strainer and placing it on a paper napkin. "Sugar?"

"Yes. Why?"

"I don't need to explain," Mark said. "One or two spoons?"

"One," Jules said, with a finality to it.

They sipped the tea—Mark without sugar, as Mark knew it was supposed to be taken. If the ginseng had its desired revitalizing effect on them, it would be the worst time for it. The silence was unbearable.

Mark felt shamed into turning his eyes. When he was busy with music, recording, and tours, he never even read the letters. Some agency just mailed them a glossy of him and his keyboard, all ripped leather and spiky brush hair and mirror shades, standing underneath a lonely streetlight near a pier, like a hustler.

"I'm sorry," Mark said, all of a sudden. "I can be very condescending."

"I thought you'd be different."

"How?"

"I'm probably not that gay, I'm not so hung up about my fuckin' mail."

"It's just me, then."

"It's not just you, it's all of this," Jules said. "All this fuckin' hide and seek. If you people weren't so full of shit, with your stupid lifestyle, and made it so hard for the rest of us, I'd probably be living with a guy now."

"I'm pretty ordinary."

"Not when I'm sticking it up your ass."

That flew by so quickly it made Mark shudder. Mark hadn't seen that one coming.

"It's a hard life," Mark said. "People won't back off. That's why I don't make music anymore."

"Oh yeah?"

"I can't understand why it's so important that they have to know."

"I don't know either. . . . My wife and I were at a party last week. She made all these fag jokes, as if she were talking to me in front of these people. . . . It slips out when you least expect it, like's she's got evidence against me in her pocket. . . ."

"So you think she knows?"

"I think so," Jules said. "Anybody ever catch you?"

Mark stopped to consider what to reveal, and if he should.

"You don't have to if you don't want to," Jules said.

"There was this colleague of mine," Mark said. "Pretty open about it, I didn't resent him for it. But he was so bent on dragging people out in the open, I don't know why. We were at a bar, all the record people and the band and me, and this guy just said, in front of me, out loud for everyone to hear: 'Mark *has* to be gay, someone who writes songs like that *has* to be gay.' He was trying to provoke me. I almost punched his face in. I was just so in love with him, and I was waiting for the right moment, for when we would have privacy, for me to bring him home with me and show him who I really was. Because I found his openness so attractive."

"You fall in love?"

"Not anymore," Mark said. "I'll never be open, especially if assholes like him get to feel good about themselves because I'm like them."

"I don't know," Jules said. "I don't get it with angry faggots. What did you say to him?"

"I said nothing, and somebody changed the subject quickly."

Mark noticed that his cup was empty. He quietly offered Jules a refill by lifting his tea strainer. Jules nodded.

"I hate it," Mark said.

"This gay thing?"

"No. That I silenced myself into oblivion."

Mark refilled his cup.

"'Silenced myself into oblivion,'" Jules reiterated, sugaring his tea. "I like how that sounds."

"So do the people who write to me," Mark said. "Not exactly what I felt."

"So you were faking it?"

"I never really said anything to begin with."

It was so very uncomfortable. Mark wanted to keep things like this a closed issue. He never thought that his sex life—once anonymous, now more personable if discreet—would ever ask him to open up like this. He just wanted to be wanted for himself, not for what he felt or thought or did. And yet to acquiesce, to give full access to someone else seemed desirable, and even necessary, in moments when his heart was really in it—usually when he was meditating on it while fixing a house, alone.

"Well . . . I didn't come here to talk," Jules said, taking Mark's forearm. "I'm not here to figure out my life, or figure out yours."

"Please. Continue."

"I'm sorry to have pushed it. I should have respected your privacy."

"Someone's got to push the envelope," Mark said.

Mark pushed the letters to Jules's side of the table, putting a good, humbled face on.

Jules just glanced at them, not really reading them, like

glancing at a memo to see if it had something to say to him. By the time Jules sped through a few of them, Mark had cleared the table of his mug, rinsed the mug and the teapot, and set them to dry on a wooden dish rack.

"So?" Mark said.

"These kids must not have much of a life," Jules said. "What kind of a freak would write something like this?"

"I was afraid you'd say that," Mark said.

"Why?"

Because I am like those kids. "They're pretty weird," Mark said. "It's getting very hot in here. . . . Let me lend you a pair of shorts and a T-shirt."

"Okay," Jules said.

When Mark tried the shorts-and-T-shirt gambit on men he wasn't sure were in the mood, they never got a chance to try them on once they undressed.

It also worked this time.

ii.

Jan 6, 198-

Dear Mr. Mark Piper:

I hope my letter gets to you somehow.

I am a big fan of yours. When is your next record coming out? Will your old records be out on CD? (I just bought a used CD player. I've been buying most of my favorite stuff on CD since, wish is OK, since I don't have a lot of favoreites.) I haven't found anything at the record store; they just have *Ghosts,* your first album (in cassette). I miss having new music from you. None of the other kids in school listen that much to you lately. You are too "wierd". I like "wierd" music, and "wierd" vidios. I guess I'm pretty "wierd".

I think I am your biggest fan. I have everything

of yours. I say I "love" your music, like I would love someone. I listen to your music and I feel at home. I read the lirics on the sleeves and sometimes, when I hear the songs, they make me cry.

I have a hard time explaining how your songs feel to me. It's like you sing the songs of my life, like my life is a movie and your songs are the songs in the soundtrack album. (I'm wierd!) I once even dressed up for Halloween as you. You say things for me that I cannot say like you say them. Like when I love somebody, it's like your songs say. And when I'm sad or angry or confused I feel like you feel, and I don't know what that means, like your songs say. And when I hear your music I don't feel so wierd or lonely, because I think if you met me you would like me and understand me. Because I understand the ghosts in your music:

"Silenced into oblivion
got too many things to hide
pain that I've been given
pain I've got inside
ghosts inside my pockets
shadow traces deep inside me
necessary clouds inside me
necessary clouds inside."

Please make more records.
Sincerely,
Anthony French
Cincinnati, OH

iii.

Now it was as if he had jumped off the plane with all the thrill of the risk and the feeling of falling and the ground moving so fast toward him, and him ready to let his parachute unfurl and let his feet touch the ground. But now, as soon as he jumped off the airplane, gravity stopped, and he just stayed still, in midair, with nowhere to go, unable to land, desperate for that endless floating to be over, desperate to touch land, touch what was real, if there were only land underneath him—

Mark streched on his back, his legs pulled tight to his chest, as Jules slowly entered him, the first feelings of penetration always uncomfortable, then that feeling of being full instead of empty, then, once in, Jules went in and out of him and the unspeakable ardor was not there. Just the discomfort, just the feeling of being perforated like tissue paper. It was like shitting backwards, not a trace of that gut feeling of being loved and wanted and pleasured.

Mark looked beyond Jules's face, which was straining with sweat and effort, at the ceiling, and it was as if he were really up there, watching himself with a cold eye, a strange feeling of being disembodied, as if Jules were fucking his body but not him, as if he were letting his body be usurped, but his spirit was not here with him, his body was hollow, just meat.

And the strange thing was that Mark had initiated sex, as if he wanted it after all—as if he *should* want it. Because that was enough. Being fucked by someone who was less of a stranger was a consolation prize for not finding love, and certainly better than being fucked by a stranger. And yet didn't he let him in, into the privacy of his home, even let him look at things that he'd rather keep private, things that it hurt to reveal? Didn't he let him inside him?

There was something fundamentally wrong with this, and he couldn't put his finger on it—wait, Jules was catching on that his heart wasn't in it. Mark moaned and begged to be fucked harder, even though Jules was going at it as he had in the past.

And in the past, hadn't it been pleasurable that he'd

found someone reasonably right for him, with a minimum of haranguing about it? The thrill of it, the first few months; it was immensely pleasurable to be overwhelmed by this man.

Now there was something missing that hadn't been missing before.

And he could see Jules's face grimace and feel Jules's roar growing slowly inside him, and Mark remembered to fake it, to fake the pleasure, to stretch and moan and clench his jaws and his bowels in rhythm as if he too were coming from being fucked.

Even though he didn't feel anything but some uncomfortable physical sensations.

Jules came inside him. With a few thrusts, each one deeper and slower and more finally exhausting than the next, Jules became still, and leaned down to kiss Mark.

"You're *so* hot," Jules said.

"You're hot, too," Mark said.

Mark still floated in the air, above ground masked by clouds that would not break. He breathed in silence for a few minutes while they cuddled, horrified by how easily he could deny himself, deny his feelings the dignity of their own truth, and pretend that their denial could erase any trace of what they revealed to him about himself, as if he could make their gravity seem not all that real, as if this lie was better than knowing in full, undeniable clarity what the shame and pain was all about. But the illusion that this man, that *any* man could really fullfill him through sex just couldn't be maintained any longer.

The clouds broke. Maybe he was truly the weird one, the one unable to live like everyone else, with their secrets, their hypocrisies, their lies, their distractions, their easy satisfactions, all because he was a man and engaged in this kind of sex. It was not the kind of sex, but the kind of love he wanted that disturbed him. The ghost of an idea, the idea of being a man and wanting to love and be loved by a man filled him with far more shame than just sex. And nothing could fulfill him in the face of such an inexplicable, impossible love. And mere sex, in the face of this unresolvable longing, was worse than mere loneliness.

The clouds broke, and he fell and finally touched ground.

Losing Count

Late at night, at the convenience store, Edward keeps himself busy listening to the TV while watching small-town thugs walk by in twos and threes to unknown destinations. He can't help but feel a certain kind of passionate curiosity about them: what their lives are about, what they do, what they think, if they'd be all right with him if he'd made some gesture of interest. When they come inside to pay for gas or buy beer or cigarettes, he treats them with the same hardened, indifferent expressions they share with him. In the store, they seem more like discharged military boys than unemployed skinheads. Ed catalogues and withholds his desire for these drifters; it keeps him alive and awake at 3:00 in the morning. It steals a bit of abundance inside this state of limitations.

Ed's stealth also provides for pocket money. He punches into the cash register only part of any given purchase—he enters a pack of cigarettes but not the six-pack of beer bought along with them—and keeps the difference between what the customer pays and what the roll registers. He quickly runs the proper subtotals and taxes in his head to give the customer correct change and no time to notice any irregularity in the transaction.

It all adds up to about $500 a week in cash—more than equal to his biweekly salary. No one keeps proper inventory of the convenience store's items; he's been shorting the register for a couple of years and hasn't ever been caught.

The clunk of bottles on the counter drags him away from looking outside the window. The harsh lighting in the store, which shines off dusty candy-bar wrappers and freezers clouded with condensation, bothers Ed's eyes as he tries to focus on another customer: a tall, slightly portly, unpretentious man dressed in outdoorsman's clothes the color of party favors instead of camouflage. The customer places a six-pack of beer on the counter with an almost hostile hurry. The aroma of percolating coffee fights with leaking freon for the smell of the moment.

"A pack of Luckies, please. Can you make change for a hundred?" the customer asks. "I'm out of small bills."

"Sure," Ed says. Ring in the Luckies. Pack of Luckies, six-pack, tax, total. Take the bill.

Ed holds the crisp bill up to the light.

"Cute guys, aren't they," the customer says.

"I'm sorry?"

"The guys across the street. You were looking at them."

"I don't know what you're talking about." Ed sticks the hundred under the till and starts to pull out a few twenties but he's lost count.

"I know what I'm talking about, you just go and pretend that I don't."

The TV set murmurs about a sale on camcorders; with only minutes to go before the next product, the pitchman suggests you could use the camera to protect your children from the cruelty of baby-sitters.

"What's the hurry?" the customer says. "It's not like the store's busy." Ed bags the items, looks out of the window again as if it's a meaningless habit. The customer counts the money.

"I think you've given me too much change back," the customer says, showing his dainty yellowed canines with a smile.

"Did I?"

"It looks like you didn't charge me for the beer."

"I didn't mean to."

"Are you giving away free beer?"

"I meant I didn't mean to not charge you for the beer."

"I know it's hard to keep your mind on things." The customer hands him a ten. "My name's Gardner. When does your shift end? There's this place I want to take you to."

Gardner and Ed have breakfast at a diner Ed hasn't visited before. Firemen from the nearby station have the three-egg special. The diner looks like the dining car on a train that just happened to stop and stay where it was; the chrome details on the booths and counters suggest the energy of flight while staying still and growing dull. Ed cases the place, hoping there's no one here who might know him.

"Check that one out, isn't he beautiful?" Gardner says, pointing quickly and covertly in the right direction.

"Very much," Ed says.

"So why haven't you left town?"

"My family lives here. You?"

"It's a safe place for me to pursue my trade, I suppose. How did a good-looking guy like you end up in a convenience store?"

"I've made it work for me."

"I've noticed," Gardner says.

"Do you have anything better for me?"

"I'll keep my eyes open for you."

"I used to have my own business, you know."

"Really?"

"A stationery store. Then the factories left town," Ed says. "No factory, no greeting cards sold."

"I think this town's going to turn around soon."

"I imagine."

"You gotta believe it. Live with your family?"

"No. But they're in town. You?"

"They're both dead."

"Did you kill them?"

"God, no, I liked them way too much. But I appreciate you asking," Gardner says. "Oh, man, check the shoulders on that one. He's standing up now."

The fireman tucks his shirt into his pants, his shoulder blades resisting the cloth; rolls of muscle bunch up around his broad neck.

"Very nice," Ed says.

"Do you like to look at me, too?"

Gardner's eyes, blue with yellow flecks and a greenish tint around the iris, stay put on Ed's. The odor of burning eggs, so mundane after years of daily exposure, becomes suggestive, urgent.

"Yes," Ed says.

"I like looking at you, too."

Gardner reams himself on Ed so hard it's like Gardner wants to fuck all of Ed into his ass. Gardner grabs Ed's chin when he notices he's not being looked at. Gardner tells Ed to to hang on, to grab him hard. They wind down in sweaty sheets, Ed gently rubbing the scratches on Gardner's arms as he falls asleep.

Ed wakes up alone, late in the afternoon, looks around wondering if anything's missing from the apartment. The appliances, the compact discs, the wallet, the computer, nothing's missing. He finds a square engraving plate the size of a chocolate bar on top of the unopened mail on the kitchen table. Gardner's name and out-of-state number stand out in regal, small-capped letters; Ed feels the etched grooves around them, sharp enough to feel like they could cut his skin. Didn't he say he was local? Ed's annoyed that he slept with another out-oftowner, but he thinks of calling him, even for just a fuck if he gets lonely.

A few shifts later, Ed stops mopping the floor when he notices a small man in a tired blue suit has entered the store and stopped before the Wet Floor sign. Ed returns to his position in the cashier's booth; the man follows him, avoiding hollows in the linoleum that haven't quite dried, and pulling an ID wallet out of his jacket with a thick-fingered hand as if it were a shield. Squat but wide, his hair thin and gray and badly cut, the fed leans on the edge of the half-empty ice-cream freezer that keeps all customers just short of arm's length from the counter.

"Good morning," the detective says, snapping his badge closed.

"Let me look at that," Ed says. The detective hands over the wallet with an ink-stained hand. Special Agent, Federal Bureau of Investigation. The fed appears to be pleased with himself in the picture, better dressed, as if he hadn't yet lost the desire to look good in a suit.

"My name's Vince," the fed says.

"Don't you always come in twos?" Ed asks.

"You're clever," Vince says. "My partner's otherwise busy. Is this a good time to talk?"

"As good as any," Ed says.

"I'll make it short and sweet: my partner and I have been tracking a counterfeiter who's been passing hot hundred-dollar bills around for the last few weeks. I understand you run this shift on Mondays?"

"Yes."

"Last Tuesday, one of the phony bills showed up in this store's cash count. The bank reported it to us."

"I'm sorry to hear that," Ed says.

"Do you recall making change for a hundred-dollar bill last Monday night?"

"I think I might have. Not sure."

Vince walks over to the candy rack, picks up a caramel crunch bar, and dusts it off against the arm of his jacket. "I looked at the receipt rolls for Monday night. You did accept a hundred-dollar bill." Vince puts the bar back on the display.

"Then why did you ask?"

"Just a habit. I don't want to overlook anything."

"You already knew," Ed says.

"I also looked at the surveillance tape."

"Really. Surveillance tape."

"It's interesting. You spend a lot of time looking out of a window."

"Would you blame me with a job like this?"

"No, I wouldn't. Everybody has to find a way to feed his family. Young man like you, probably married with a baby or two."

The ice machine shudders into life, lets go of another shower of ice cubes.

"I'm queer," Ed says.

"Queer?"

"I'm queer."

"As a three-dollar bill?"

"I suppose."

"As a Christmas goose?"

"What's it to you?"

Vince leans over the ice-cream freezer and stares at Ed. Vince just as quickly turns away. "I'm sorry, I didn't want to push it," Vince says. "I always have to try —"

"It must be a habit."

"You've got me all figured out. You know, there's this moment in the surveillance tape where you lose count. You were counting a *lot* of money. Do you remember?"

"Maybe I should see this tape."

"That's not a bad idea. How much for a Squishee?" The fed puts a buck down on the counter.

In a small room at the local police station, Vince plays back the sequenced, black-and-white snapshots of Ed making change for a hundred, and then for a ten. Vince's partner sits calmly in the dark behind them while Vince walks around Ed, hands in pockets.

"I slept with him," Ed says.

"Is he a lover of yours?" Vince asks.

"No. Just a casual thing."

"Good to know."

"I have his name and number at home."

"Fabulous."

Vince's partner snorts.

"Yeah, that's funny," Vince says.

"He gave me a ten back because I hadn't rung his beer. He'd distracted me."

"That's how he works," the partner says.

"Look, I don't want him to find out I told on him."

"Was he a good lover?" Vince asks.

"Why do you want to know?"

"Well, it did take you some effort to let me know about him."

"That had nothing to do with it. I'll give a statement. Just don't let him know I told you. Please."

"I'll do what I can," Vince says.

"We appreciate your cooperation," the partner says, rising from his chair into the light of the television, the image onscreen stuck on the moment when the cash register opened a second time. The partner grabs Vince's shoulder and they walk out of the room. The playback machine shuts down automatically after holding the freeze frame for far too long.

Ed tells the whole story a few times until all the authorities are satisfied. Vince and his partner drive Ed home with a couple of local cops to pick up the evidence. The cops and the partner leave with the plate in a sealed plastic bag. Vince appears not to want to leave, leaning on the edge of the kitchen table, his tie slightly askew, flopping out of his jacket like a loose tongue. Ed shifts the clutter of expensive kitchenware on the counters; he starts to make breakfast just to take up the time. Ed finds himself making portions for two on a set of copper cookware he'd recently acquired by mail order.

"You know, it's stupid, but I think he was just trying to romance you," Vince says.

"How so?" Ed asks.

"Pretty stupid way to try to impress someone you want to sleep with. The engraving plate gives it away. Did it ever cross your mind? Honestly?"

"I knew he wanted something. Can I get you . . . do you want me to take your coat?"

"I'm fine for the moment. How good are you at math?"

"Pretty good."

"You must be good to keep all the math straight," Vince says.

"He made me lose count." Ed takes the frying pan away from the flame while still fluffing the scrambled eggs.

Vince unbuttons his suit jacket and shrugs it off his body; the gun holster makes his shoulders look especially wide and bulky as he folds the jacket on the back of chair.

"Nice place you have here," Vince says. "You live well."

"Thank you," Ed says. "I make do."

"We all make do. It's a really strange thing; you feel a strange loyalty to people you desire just because, just because you desire them. You want to protect them because you want them. And you let things pass unnoticed."

"You know, I've got nothing more to say. I've said

everything I know and I remember. There's nothing more to drag out of me."

"I wasn't talking about you," Vince says.

The scrambled eggs have become dry and rubbery. The gun in Vince's holster shines like it's just been oiled, or never used. Outside the window, it's still morning.

Property Values

i.

There wasn't anything short of a shantytown shack that Claudia Ferrier had not scouted as a property that could benefit from her skills as a realtor. That some of these dwellings had people still living in them who had no intention of relocating was another matter altogether. Such were her ambitions that, at a wake for an acquaintance's mother, she asked the bereaved if the departed's lovely four-bedroom house was going to be up for sale.

In that booming year of 1988, Claudia operated out of Mireya, the medium-sized city that served as the hub for the west coast of Puerto Rico. Her mother rode shotgun as she drove around the nicer neighborhoods of the area, and around neighborhoods with major gentrification potential, often late into the night. They looked for For Sale and For Rent signs the way some look for guavas in other people's backyards—with stealth and no intention of being neighborly. Of course, she was all pulpy sweetness when she called the phone numbers posted on oak or mahogany doors, or on the steel grillwork that enclosed most self-respecting upper middle-class porches. And people always took her calls. This was how she came to represent other people's properties. Sometimes buyers contacted her before she had a suitable property available. She would do her fieldwork and find them one.

Her wardrobe was never short of style or brand-name designers, for this hustling of buyer and seller, in a seller's market, made for more than a decent living. Especially since she charged a fee to both buyer and seller. Claudia Ferrier had not heard of any regulation against this practice in the Commonwealth of Puerto Rico and nobody had openly questioned her business methods. Before she swooped onto the scene, most people had handled real estate issues without a middleman. By the time she attempted to discourage Dean Rodriguez from acquiring a home, Claudia had gained a reputation among the *cognoscenti* of Mireya as a relatively harmless nuisance whose greed and malfeasance were tolerable. Harsher opinions saw her as the ambulance chaser of real estate agents.

ii.

The old-landed-gentry-turned-professional-money women's auxiliary—the *cognoscenti di tutti cognoscenti,* really—met for breakfast once a week. Three times a month, lavish breakfasts were held in the privacy of one of the social-club members' houses. Thick potato and onion omelettes, guava or mango jelly-filled confections dusted with the finest powdered sugar, crisp yet flaky pastry fingers filled with sweet cheese would accompany conversation whose intimacy and warmth belied the snobbery accorded to the group's members by the larger social whirl of the town. Gossip did pass among the ladies, of course, but it wasn't all frivolous. The group had a hand in all kinds of fundraising for worthy causes, got involved in library drives and literacy campaigns, and took care of the housebound elderly and infirm who had no extended family to look after them. They played canasta with Spanish playing cards; they had an unspoken, ongoing top-this! competition involving breakfast comestibles. They wished their children to marry into one another's families, and always planned major social events around their core group. But they were, actually, very sweet and conscientious in a cautiously progressive way. They tried to better themselves and their town, and they were sincere.

Once a month, though, the breakfast club met in a restaurant or a coffee shop. Claudia, knowing that these people were the shapers of good taste and public opinion, desperately wanted to become a member of this elite. After all, the group included the wife of the town's most prestigious architect of luxurious houses and apartment buildings, the wife of the most reliable and well-liked appraiser of land value and property, the wife of the financier who approved most of the loans that went into the large-scale building of homes, in addition to the wives of doctors, lawyers, and sundry professionals at the top of their fields, all of whom invested in real estate. A lot of business was done inside this group. Claudia wanted to be part of it. But she knew that a bald-faced request to be invited would lack propriety. So, on Thursday mornings—their usual meeting time—she would check all the possible breakfast venues, hoping to casually pop in to say hi at the table, be invited to sit down, and stay all morning. And then pop in often enough to feel she had arrived and invite them to breakfast at her place the next week.

On this momentous morning, she finally found the group breakfasting at the coffee shop of the chichi department store in town, the place with the best teeny-tiny cupful of strong, bitter coffee.

"What a coincidence!" Claudia said, hovering over the table, to the few who looked up from the group to acknowledge her presence. "I was just coming over here for a quick bite to eat before showing a house to a very nice couple . . . and I find you all gathered here!"

"Well, it was just a matter of time," said Olivia, the wife

of the reliable and well-liked appraiser. Claudia had had the opportunity to become acquainted with Olivia when her husband did a small appraisal job for her. "The world is a handkerchief, isn't it? How is your mother?"

"Fine, fine," Claudia said, still hovering, her hand suggestively holding onto the back of an unoccupied chair. "With her usual aches and pains. But she's such pleasant company, not a burden at all. She makes my life so much easier, truly. She really helps out with my business."

"Well, it's nice to hear your mother's doing well," Olivia said. "So nice of you to stop and say hello." Olivia smiled politely but not widely and turned to speak to another member of the party.

Claudia hovered over the table, at last reaching the point where she could no longer bear the embarrassment of being ignored, when another voice rose up to her from the coop.

"Actually—Claudia, isn't it?—maybe you could sit down for a bit and give me a little help with something."

Luisa, the doctor's wife. . . . What an opportunity, what an opening! Claudia quickly swept to her side.

"How could I serve you?" Claudia asked.

"I've been looking for a house for my son, and I am at a loss as to how to help him."

"But you, you know so much about houses! Surely you don't need any help from an *arriviste* like myself!"

"Oh, but Dean is so fussy. He was a fussy eater as a child," Luisa said.

"Was he?" Claudia said. "Poor thing."

"You see, his tastes are . . . extravagant and specific, and I haven't been able to locate something he'd like. He's looking for a castle in the air, and I haven't been able to please him. And I'm going on a trip to Europe very shortly and won't come back for two weeks or so, and Dean wants to move in before Christmas. . . . Could he call you for help? He doesn't like stucco. Everything I've seen has stucco."

iii.

"Something *must* be wrong," Claudia said to her mother while driving around in the middle of the night. They were driving through San Sebastián, a small town to the north-east of Mireya, on their hunt for signage. "Luisa could not possibly need any help from me. Luisa, the wife of the head surgeon of, at last count, three hospitals in the county, is a canny investor. She must make as a landlord at least as much as her husband. And she's sold locations downtown to fast-food concerns, and she owns parking lots and houses on the best locations in town."

"Who gave you this information?" asked her mother.

"Town records, registered deeds and such," she said. "It's all written down on paper, if you care to find it. Any-way, I just don't get it. What would she need me for? All the signs indicate that I'm being taken advantage of."

"Maybe she's doing you a favor, out of kindness."

"Hah! I don't need her *noblesse oblige*," Claudia said. "But at least she's giving me business. . . ."

"That's all that matters, doesn't it—stop!" her mother said. "I think I saw a sign."

They backed up.

The house had a few patches of faded paint that had once been a rather fetching kingfisher blue. A cement base held up a wooden structure, two floors high. The long, wide porch ran from the side of the house that opened to the side street and around a rounded corner to the side that faced the main thoroughfare of the town. The porch was framed by lovingly fluted columns and intricate, leaf-shaped latticework, some of which had fallen sideways onto the floor. The front doors had wooden slats that opened and closed to let light and air in, and on the second floor the windows that faced the side street were made in a similar manner. The top story opened up to a small balcony above the porch. The roof was flat, like most roofs in the tropics, but the edges curved out slightly, embroidered with sinuous, florid arabesques, joining at the corner to meet a horn of plenty that poured forbidden fruit.

There was no stucco on the house. No stucco whatsoever.

"What a trashy little house," Claudia said.

"Shall I write down the number?" her mother asked, pen and paper ready.

"No," she said. "Who'd want this? Only to tear it down. And who wants to live near the center of town anymore? To live near the transvestites who hang around the plaza at night? Forget it. This has no potential. Let's go near the mall. Property values are higher there."

iv.

The next morning, she got a call from Dean, Luisa's son.

"Thank you so much for taking my call," Dean said. "I don't want to impose on you and on your friendship with my mother, but I need help finding a house for myself."

Claudia was properly flattered by the fact that he called her his mother's friend. All that worry for nothing! "I am here to serve you," she said. "Where are you calling from?"

"Upstate New York."

"Oh! Maybe you can help me improve my English. I've always wanted to be a polyglot. Shall we speak English?"

"Sure," Dean said, switching tongues.

"What an enchanting young man!"

"I'm not so young, Doña Claudia."

"Call me Claudia," she said. "Well, your mother tells me that you are looking for a home."

"Not just any home," Dean said. "I've driven Mom crazy. You see, I've made my living in antiques and collectibles, and I'm . . . retiring, so I want to keep some of the things I really like . . . and I can't just place all my things in a place that doesn't *go* with them. My mother sent me snapshots of these houses that, well . . . they're a bit *too* modern."

"Something traditional?"

"Not exactly. I'd love a townhouse with a turn-of-the-century feel. You know, classy yet exuberant. Like . . . how do I explain it to you? You know, like an Aubrey Beardsley illustration."

"I am not familiar with her."

"Him," Dean said, "I guess. Anyway . . . you know Art Nouveau? Toulouse Lautrec?"

"Oh, yes! I can see it now. Art Nouveau. Very decorative."

"That's it. I want a house with that feel."

"That's going to be difficult."

"But oh so worth it. . . . I don't know, I'm very picky with details."

"It's going to be difficult to find a propriety like that."

"It's the kind of *property* I'm looking for. Price is no object. But I am a little short of time, and I'd like to move down to the island as soon as possible."

"A townhouse, though? Maybe it is too large a place for one person."

"Don't worry, I'm going to share it with someone. We both need lots of space. And I expect to have lots of houseguests over from the States, and have my family stay over for weekends. . . ."

"Ooh, a friend? You have someone living with you?" What a piece of gossip! She hadn't heard that Luisa's son was living with someone. Maybe a wedding was in the offing? Surely she would be invited now.

"Well . . . yeah. My partner. . . . He used to restore houses on the side, so if the house needs a lot of work, not to worry. Mark likes a challenge."

"Partner?" That killed the wedding idea.

"Yeah. We met when I was buying pieces for a house, and he was restoring it. We've been . . . business partners and friends since. He's gone back to the music business— he's a record producer—but he still does a little rebuilding work here and there. Me, I just buy things, but he makes them."

"Maybe your friend can do some work for me . . . for some of my clients. You maybe have not heard, but the Luna section of Mireya is being redeveloped. You know, it was once a nice neighborhood. . . . Well, the latest is, the wealthy young, they take these old houses and remake them to their taste. So now it's becoming a nice neighborhood again, though, for *my* taste, it is too close to the university. . . ."

"Maybe you can find me something of that sort?" Dean asked.

"Let's see what I can do," she said. "Anything else you have in mind?"

"I want a nice big porch, and please, no stucco!"

V.

The first thing that Claudia noticed when she saw Dean was how thin and sickly he looked. Then she saw how tenderly Dean and Mark argued about who would carry a small piece of luggage out of the baggage-claim area. And she noticed how they touched, casually flaunting their desire for each other.

As she stood by the Plexiglas divider that separated the arriving from the receiving, she decided to pretend she was waiting for someone else. Dean had homosexual AIDS! And he'd brought his fornicator with him! She didn't know how to hide herself and wished she could make herself invisible. However, she forced herself to continue smiling and looked at a young couple who had arrived on the same flight as if they were the ones she was waiting for. She kept looking at them while the plot came to her in a flash: Luisa was giving her what she herself did not want to deal with. A homosexual son! Of course, no one would like to sell to or buy from degenerates. That's why Luisa dropped him on her. *She* wouldn't look like she approved or abetted him; her reputation would be clean. But Claudia wasn't about to do Luisa a favor that would dirty her reputation. Look: Claudia sells houses to degenerates. Look: Claudia brings down property values. Look: Claudia brings the horses of the apocalypse to your neighborhood—

"Doña Claudia?"

Claudia pretended not to hear.

"Excuse me, Doña Claudia?"

Claudia had never been put in such a situation. Yes, life had ugly things, but she thought she'd left them behind when she left South America.

"Doña Claudia, it's me, Dean."

"Call me Claudia," she said turning around, a toothy smile on her face.

Before her stood Dean, in a white long-sleeved shirt, gray slacks, and wingtips. He held in the crook of his arm a winter jacket lined with the most amazing and unidentifiable fur. He looked as if a wind could lift him away. His friend Mark had the mien of yet another unremarkably cornstalk-tall American man: jeans, blue jersey shirt, Converse canvas shoes. And a ski jacket.

"It's me, Dean Rodriguez," he said, and he held a hand out in peace.

She shook it, practically trembling. She resisted the urge to wipe her hand in horror.

"This is Mark Piper," Dean said. Mark mumbled a hello

and shook her hand coldly, keeping his scary grimace. "He's kinda shy," Dean whispered.

As if that mattered to her.

Now she faced the indignity of having to force herself to speak to the homosexuals while looking at them in the eye.

"Where did you get those shoes?" Claudia said.

"Schenectady," Mark said.

vi.

Claudia had had a few properties in mind before their arrival. She did not show them to the couple. While she shifted her comfy seat cover to the shotgun seat, with the pretense of making Dean comfortable—she could burn the seat cover later and avoid contamination—she wondered what to do. She would subtly discourage the dregs from buying anything by showing them dregs. But where would she take them? This question did not remain unanswered for long, for Claudia had a prodigious memory for properties. She recalled the house in San Sebastián. Genius! she thought. Who'd buy that filthy thing? Meanwhile, there was the matter of preparing them for a disappointment.

"Oh, it was so hard to find something to suit you!" Claudia said, practicing her English. "I am afraid that houses like the ones you like have been torn down."

"What a pity," Dean said. "I've always wanted to live in one. My grandmother had one. When I was five years old, she hired someone to wreck it and build a cement thing in its place."

"Funny how your mother couldn't find you one," she said. "She buys so many houses. . . ."

"Yeah," Dean said. "My mother collects houses like I collect cookie jars. But, well, my mother's tastes run to the conventional, and I just couldn't live in something like that."

"If you pardon me asking," she said, "why do you wish to move to the island?"

"Can I speak with you in the strictest confidence?"

"Not a problem," she said. Her curiosity was stronger than her distaste. Besides, this would be great currency in the gossip exchange.

"Well, I'm going to pass away, so I hope to spend my last few years in my native land. Mark agreed to take a year or two off and move here with me. . . . So it's a matter of finding the perfect place for me and all of my things."

"Oh, you are deadly sick?"

"Don't I look it?"

"Not at all! I just thought you were a vegetarian or something."

Mark, in the backseat, somehow found this awfully funny. Why, she was just being nice.

They drove by the main plaza of San Sebastián. It was a late Tuesday afternoon. Sadly, Claudia noted, there was no suggestion of the town loonies, drug addicts, drag queens, and indigents that would congregate there at nightfall.

"Here we are," she said, with a slight sigh, as if this house was the best she could find. She stepped out of the car. Mark stepped out and opened the door for Dean. Now those two, Claudia thought with piercing irony, are perfect little gentlemen. . . .

She stood in front of the house with absolute stillness and gravity, as if she were pondering a great injustice, noticing that the For Sale sign had fallen onto the floor of the porch. Mark and Dean soon joined her, looking at the house in silence.

A queer breeze flew through the shutters of the front door.

"It's perfect," Mark said.

What? She turned in shock to look at Mark smiling shyly, putting his arm around Dean.

"But . . . but . . . it is badly in need of disrepair!" she said.

"Mark likes a challenge," Dean said. "You should see what he did to our house in Ithaca. Shall we go in?"

Oh, Sainted Mother, she did not have the keys. It wasn't even her house to represent. She did not know to whom the house belonged. Now her charade fell apart.

She made a show of looking through her purse. "My Lord, I forgot to bring the keys with me—"

"The door's open, I think," Mark said. "May we go in?"

"Ah, well, ah . . . why not?" Claudia smiled, rictus-like.

Mark and Dean climbed up the steps to the porch. With a slight push, Mark jostled the thin doors open. Inside, ceilings rose to great heights, wallpaper fell and folded over the floor, dust accumulated. Mark felt the walls and the beams of the house like a doctor palpating for unseemly bumps in glandular regions. Dean followed his own path into the house, going straight to the kitchen in the back. Claudia followed Dean, hoping to help him find something he didn't like. From the backyard emanated the smell of guavas rotting on moist ground. In the bare and dirty cupboard, Dean found a ceramic cookie jar in the shape of a log cabin.

"An omen," Dean said, inspecting the jar with an expert's eye. "You know they haven't made these in God knows how long. And this is in perfect shape. People just don't know what they're throwing away." He put the jar down, leaned on the countertop, and swept his eyes over the expanse of the kitchen.

"We'll take it," Dean said.

"I'll . . . I'll call you tomorrow to sign on the propriety," she said.

"Fabulous," Dean said. "Fabulous property."

"Property," she repeated. Fabulous, my foot.

Mark walked into the kitchen, an aw-gosh smile on his face, holding a player-piano roll in hand as if it were a treasure.

"Found this upstairs," Mark said, and showed it to Dean. "Does this mean something, or what?"

vii.

Claudia started a bonfire in her backyard with her mother's help, and threw the car-seat comforter, and the coffee cup she offered to Dean out of social obligation, into the flames. How could have she missed those signs? "Partner"? "Antiques"? "Upstate New York"? Dead giveaways. It could have not been clearer. And she was so desperate for a sale that she did not listen to her reason and patch those pieces of information together to figure out that he was a pervert. She couldn't shake off the feeling of having been violated somehow, even after scrubbing herself raw with a brush, à la Karen Silkwood, to make sure there was no risk of contamination. Maybe all he wanted was to move back home to torture his family with shame. Yes, revenge, the revenge of the perverse; now that he was sick with the filth of his desires he was rubbing it in the face of his family, making them watch him die slowly. No wonder his mother couldn't find him a home! And Claudia was caught in the web of that family's intrigue.

But no, she would not embroil herself in this. She would not lower herself to help those two find a home in her adopted country. Or would she? Could she find a way of selling them the house and let Luisa and her clan suffer the indignity? What would other people say! Look: what a bad mother, she had a homosexual child. Look: how her child pays her for not raising him well. Look: now she brings death and decay to our tropical paradise—

But at what cost! Claudia's reputation would look even worse. No, she would not bother to call the owners. She would call the next morning, saying the deal could not go through. Better yet, they had already accepted another offer. She would call them at the hotel where she'd dropped them off. The whole thing had so perturbed her that she had driven home with his fur-lined jacket on the backseat. She almost threw it in the fire with her things. But the fur, whose origin she couldn't place—was it fox? sable? degenerate, for sure—was too beautiful to throw into the purifying flames. She put on dishwashing gloves and stuffed it into the thickest plastic bag she could find. Maybe she would return it to Luisa as a sign that she had washed—scrubbed, really—the whole dirty affair off her hands.

The next morning, Claudia called Dean with the terrible news.

"What a sad day!" she exhaled.

"So, are we closing the deal?" Dean asked.

"Ah, I am afraid that the people who own the house, well, they are already in negotiations to sell the house."

An odd silence occurred.

"Really." Dean sounded completely unconvinced.

"Yes," she said. "A fast-food thing, you know, has been getting clearance to build there. And just yesterday they got a permit from the town government."

Another, odder silence occurred.

"And there is nothing else available that I know of—to your taste, of course. . . ." she added. "Maybe you could return home, and I could call you when I find something. . . ."

Last night's bonfire still smoldered in the backyard. The bag stuffed with the jacket lay in a cupboard in her laundry room, near and dear to her bottles of bleach.

Dean took a deep breath on the other side of the phone. "Can I tell you a quick story, Miss Claudia? It just so happens that I called my mother as soon as I got to the hotel. I told her I was delighted with the house. She told me she knew the house, that a family our family was friends with not long ago owned the house, and that a bachelor uncle of theirs lived there until he died forty years ago. And that nobody had been able to sell the house since then, that someone had said the house was jinxed, or that it had a ghost or something. Now, Mom keeps in contact with everyone she's ever met, and she told me to call her friends and say hi for her."

"Heh, the world is a handkerchief," Claudia mumbled.

"I phoned them up. They were delighted that someone wanted the house, and that it was someone that they knew personally. You see, I had dinner at their table and played with their kids when we were very young. They said they had fond memories of me. They said they would be, to use the Spanish term, *encantados* to have me over for dinner tonight and sign the papers."

"How. . . ?"

"The thing is—did I hallucinate this? Or are you lying? And if you are lying, let me tell you, I'm going to get the house no matter what."

Claudia was *incensed* that he should dare question her integrity. "The house is mine to sell, not for you to take from me!"

"By the way, I mentioned that you showed us the house, and they had absolutely no knowledge of your existence."

"It is not proper for you to go behind my back like this! The propriety is mine to sell!"

"Propriety is theft," Dean said.

Claudia heard the line go dead, and she was *furious.*

viii.

Claudia immediately called Olivia, the appraiser's wife, hoping to smear things up as much as she could with the high-grade dirt she had on Luisa's son. If she put Luisa in enough trouble, maybe she would be shamed into seclusion . . . and perhaps Luisa's place in the social order might need to be filled. . . .

"Ay, Olivia," Claudia said. "I know something so terrible . . . so terrible . . . I cannot possibly keep it secret any longer. Oh, the shame. . . ."

"What is it?"

"You know, the Rodriguezes' youngest son . . . ?"

"Dino?"

"He calls himself Dean now."

"I know."

"Well. . . . He came over to do some business with me . . . and, well. . . ."

"Yes?"

"Dean is homosexual. And he is sick with AIDS! Can you imagine, Luisa letting her son have a lifestyle like that! How could a mother let a child do that to himself?"

Today was evidently the day for odd silences.

"You heard?" Claudia said.

"No, no . . . I hadn't heard," Olivia said.

"Terrible, isn't it."

"Very sad," Olivia said. "Everyone embarks on a sad journey."

"Speaking of journeys, we must go on a shopping trip to the capital. I found the quaintest shoe store in the old city center. It's adorable; it's no bigger than a living room but their stock is imported and exclusive to the shop."

"That sounds very interesting. But right now I'm all set for shoes."

"We wouldn't just buy shoes. There's much we can talk about. Share. How about tomorrow?"

"Tomorrow we're having breakfast at my place."

"Really!"

"Yes. We're organizing a fund-raiser, and we're going to have an expert come in to help us out. He's raised funds for this cause before, and he's well-known in the community, so we're looking forward to breakfasting with him."

"Has . . . has a chair been decided for this committee?"

Claudia asked, the intricate machinery in her head spinning, spinning plots.

"Why, would you like to run it?"

"My organizational skills, if I may say so, could be an
asset to the group."

"Perhaps you should offer your help tomorrow?"

"It would be my great pleasure!"

"Fabulous," Olivia said. "I'm sure you'll fit right in. . . ."

ix.

Within the idiom of casual daytime wear for the tropics,
Claudia Ferrier dressed to impress at the breakfast. The
outfit she wore cannot be fully described without naming a
designer or two. It consisted of a blue-green silk blouse, the
slacks that came along with it as a set, accessorized with a
big dark blue belt with a silver buckle, matching shoes
with not-too-high heels, silver-mounted aquamarine ear-
rings and necklace (her emeralds would have been *too*
flashy), and a tiny little handbag that hung and swung
from her shoulder by a silver chainlet. Elegant yet colorful,
composed yet casual, classy yet friendly, serious yet fun;
why, the outfit stood for how she wanted to be seen. She
showed up slightly late to make an entrance, and be noticed, and be introduced to everyone as the glittering new
member of the family.

An entrance she surely did make. The room fell into silence as the group, one by one, turned to glare at her.

Dean sat on the center seat of the table, holding up a
cheese pastry in the air, Mark leaning over and whispering
into his ear.

How could she save this situation? Talk, quickly!

"Dean . . . ," she said, running over to his side, "Dean . . .
I am so sorry, you left your beautiful coat in my car. . . ."

"And?" Dean asked.

"Ah . . . what brings you here?"

"I'm organizing an AIDS benefit. And you, what kind of mischief are you up to?"

Dean smiled, a wide, toothy smile. Mark looked at her as if he were about to throttle her. Claudia look around to see that all eyes were upon her.

"Oh, you know Dean, how pleasant," said Olivia, from her corner of the table. "I'm so sorry Luisa is not here to see you as well."

Claudia kept trying to ingratiate herself with Dean. "Uh . . . uh . . . what kind of animal fur is your coat?" asked Claudia.

"It's cretin," said Mark.

Claudia visibly amused herself with Mark's remark. "Oh, what a funny American. . . ."

"You have no power here," Dean said. "Begone, before a house falls on you, too."

X.

Claudia left the party soon after, bursting with tears and agony. What would she tell her mother?

Flatware

I came home with red ink still wet on my fingers. That cheap pen exploded on me as I graded tests from my freshman literature course. Must have been anger, feeding through my fingertips into the pen. I felt like the Mrs. in the Scottish play, and felt even worse that it was such an inelegant and obvious metaphor for the interior life I purport to have.

I'd taken over the course from a retiring professor. It was my opportunity to prove myself and place my stamp on the syllabus, while still fulfilling the expectations of the department. But I had to accept their "suggestion" that I keep "Death in Venice" on the reading list—after all, I'm only an assistant professor. It's one step up from adjunct, so I shouldn't be complaining.

But I hate that story with a fuckin' passion: I hate the prose, I hate the voice, I hate its so-called ironic quality (irony my *foot*), I hate what the story says about human beings, and about queers in particular. And I have to use the sucky translation.

I mean, enough with stories about love and death. Scratch that, enough with stupid, superficial, and grandiose stories about love and death, especially with queers. It's a NAMBLA fantasy with Nazi overtones, and the day it goes out of print, it'll be a great day for faggots everywhere. Pardon my French.

So I was grading the tests on the train home, trying to contain my loathing for that story and be fair to my students, who'd had to put up with perhaps the lamest lecture

I've ever presented. It was only one-fourth of the test grade, anyway. To keep my interest, I positioned it with "The Dead," "Aura," and "Tlön, Uqbar, Orbis Tertius." I asked a whole heck of a lot more interesting questions about those three stories. And—in the event that I had so crippled their insight and appreciation for that abomination of a tale that they were now unable to even answer my perfunctory questions about it—I came up with an extra credit essay question that neatly went into the *gestalt* of the selections:

"Vladimir Nabokov said that art is beauty plus pity. Please choose one of the stories featured in this exam and discuss it in the context of this statement."

This question was especially neat because it dovetailed right into their next assigned reading, *Pale Fire*. I took pride in how I designed the course. It should all flow together, have a sensibility about it, rather than merely exist as a canonical list of books that 1 Should Read 2 B Edjicated.

In any event, Charlie didn't notice the ink on my fingers when he practically jumped out of bed with good news. He held me close to him. When he let go of me, my fingerprints were all over his silk kimono. Charlie said, "Oops, there's a spot."

I felt, when he held me, the little slot in the crook of his arm where an IV clips into him like a phone jack. I smelled the rubbing alcohol floating off his skin, the handiwork of Camilla and Sue, the couple who take care of him during the day when I'm away. I felt against me the reassuring layer of fat that was slowly returning to his body.

"Did you hear the news?" Charlie said.

"Calm down, sweetie," I said. "There's nothing to be that excited about."

"They've come up with a vaccine!" Charlie said.

"No shit?"

"Yeah!" Charlie said, aswoon. "News just broke on the nets. Now you can go get your shots, like a good puppy."

I couldn't articulate my surprise. That an AIDS vaccine finally had been developed. That Charlie would want me to get it. That Charlie wasn't bitter that it was not a cure for AIDS. That he'd still die, anyway, and that he'd still want me to live. That I am so in love with Charlie.

"Aren't you glad?" Charlie asked, slowly undoing my tie. "Isn't it fabulous?"

"It's unbelievable," I said, and I let him spoon me.

Spooning hadn't frightened me like that in years. I have no fear of flatware of this kind. But this was scaring the bejesus out of me.

I lost interest in spooning. 'Cause I couldn't understand what he was so happy about.

"So how was work. . . ?" I said.

That came off just a tad too condescending. I was sorry the moment I finished saying it.

"What, you don't believe me?" Charlie said, gathering his kimono around him.

"Well, sweetie," I said, digging my own grave, "it's not like this is the first time you've jumped for joy at cyber-gossip. Is this *absolutely* true?"

Charlie flashed a blank, accusatory stare and sped off to his computer room. I trudged behind him, as if cutting through a forest of thorns. I stopped at the study's open door; within, my sleeping beauty's outline glowed with the light of the outsized graphic-designer monitor. Panels shone onscreen with his design work and open text files (electronic mail, news wires, whatever).

"Is *Reuter's* trustworthy?" he said, swiveling on the desk chair.

"Not like the *New York Times,*" I said.

"You don't really trust me, then," he said.

"I'm sorry?" I said, surprised.

After I got my shot, I imagined little robots coursing through my veins, zapping malignancies. I always cutify the frightening, if I don't outright avoid it. I chose to stay away from the crowds and the mania of the big city and got my shot after the frenzy died down. I made an appointment with my doctor on campus. She takes my trimonthly tests—invariably negative—with a tact and expediency that have earned my trust. And Carla—Dr. Todd to you— doesn't buy my bullshit.

"Relax," Carla said as I began to unbutton my shirt when she walked into the cubicle. "You're getting undressed and I haven't briefed you on the risks yet."

I stopped at the third shirt button. "I just want to get this over with," I said.

"Want to talk?" she said. She gave me one of those looks that told me she knew there was more at stake for me than I pretended there was.

"Charlie wants me to take the shot," I said, "so let's do it."

I mean, I've been with Charlie for ten years now, nursing him through good periods and bad, even making love when we're both up to it, and I've remained negative. It wasn't difficult: I've only known safe sex, and Charlie was honest with me about his status when we met. When it comes to flatware (our code word for sex), it's more spooning than forking, so the shot is purely a formality. I don't really need it. I might as well take the vaccine to please my husband. Charlie's in remission right now, with a little help from some gastrointestinal technothingies. He can keep his food down, and soon he'll be graduating to eating ten-course meals, God willing. So, why do I resent getting a shot?

"Let me explain how it works first," Carla said. "This doesn't prevent AIDS as much as tame it. I'm sure you've read this in the newspaper."

"Charlie told me about it," I said.

"If you ever contract it, you'll only have a very mild case, like bouts with bronchitis or fever. But that can be medicated easily and cheaply. You're at high risk, with a sick spouse, so I heavily recommend you take it."

Charlie told me this, too. He's told me everything, everything, as if I were the one who needed to have all the facts spelled out, who needed to be encouraged and supported in my health-care choices. I decide to humor her with my attention.

"Any side effects?" I ask.

"You're a healthy guy, so it can only police your already existing immune system. Think of it as insurance," she said. "It only takes two weeks for the inoculation to yield protection. So play it safe till then. Though a lot of people go into the breach as soon as they run out of the office, I wouldn't recommend it."

Funny. It used to take two weeks for an HIV test to get graded.

"I'm in no rush," I said. "I know it's coming someday, and, well . . . I'm not that important. I don't really need it."

She put her hand on my forearm. "Don't be so morbid."

"I'm not morbid," I said. "I'm realistic."

"Would you like some Prozac with this?" Carla said.

"No," I said, sighing, letting go of my anger with a breath. "Just a little tea and sympathy."

"How's Charlie doing?"

"He's like he's taking care of me, now."

Charlie and I can't afford to refit him with a new immune system. It's incredibly expensive, and the technothingies take a long time to rebuild what Nature hath wrought and make him fully functional. So we don't have the time either.

It's not that we've stopped struggling against his condition. I couldn't earn enough for both of us, so Charlie sold his insurance with the help of a broker friend when debt got out of hand. That makes Charlie an investment that yields when it goes bust. But Charlie can enjoy his life insurance now, when he's alive. Death futures investors don't know that we're cheating death a little bit. We used the money for some "amenities" (as Charlie calls them), like the technothingies in his stomach lining. They've kept him well enough to absorb his tubloads of medicine and eat well. And the transfusions of blood don't have to carry all the burden of his survival.

The night after I got my shot, I found enough fat on his belly for me to grasp and fondle. Oh, God, it was magic.

Carla put down her yellow legal pad. "Oh, please, Serge."

"I'm not kidding!" I said. "He's talked so much about the whole fuckin' thing, it's as if it's going to make him better!"

Carla sighed, stood up, and picked up this elongated staple gun from the side of a slick-wheeled console. I felt as if she were going to pump me full of gas.

"If you don't know what's going on, I'm not going to be the one to tell you," she said. "Take off your shirt."

I had never been so terrified of being naked.

"I'm *only* going to last so long," Charlie said. "If you get the vaccine, maybe you can look for someone else after I go."

"Jesus!" I said. "Let's just drop it."

Charlie sliced vegetables into pleasant shapes and I perspired over stew and noodles. The ink stains on his robe were quite flattering, really.

"Nothing, Serge," he said. "I just want you to think about yourself, for a change."

"Look, I've sown my wild oats. What if I want to spend the rest of my life as a widow?"

"That's so sweet. Get me a barf bag," he said.

Charlie's strange in that he looks like Ernest Hemingway, thinks like Oscar Wilde, and seamlessly goes from butch to swish, sometimes within the same sentence.

"I don't know, Charlie. I just feel you're pushing me into this decision."

"So, I want you to live."

"Not if you fuckin' can't."

"Gee, I've lasted ten years, sky's the limit now. Why do you have to spend your days worried if you're going the same way, too?"

"I've handled it till now."

"You won't have to anymore."

"Oh, is it that you want to have plain old unsafe sex, is that it?"

Charlie pointed at me with the cutting knife. Oh, shit. "It really hurts to hear that that's what you think this is all about. Though it's nice to see you putting up a fight."

"Why?"

"Do you know what it is to be married to a martyr?"

"So, tie me to a tree and pierce me dead with a bow and arrow."

"Why do you make this so difficult?" he asked.

I don't know.

The vegetables were not quite so elegantly cut at this point in the conversation. He dropped the knife. He stood up with a steadiness and determination that almost had me cry miracle, or call for help. I dropped the cooking spoon inside the stewpot. Can the ill kill?

No. They come over to you slowly, and sidle up to you, and take you and kiss you gently.

And you drop your arms, and your defenses, and you cry.

And they let you mourn them while they're still alive.

"Will you do this for me?" he said.

"Yes," I said. "Yes, I will, yes."

"I will *never* understand why it takes you so long to take my word for anything," he said.

There once was a time when it seemed that time would just stretch into infinity, and that I could love someone so strongly, so powerfully, that the world would bend to my love, and nothing would ever hurt him, because I said so.

That time is gone.

"I'm sorry, I'm just so wiped out," I said. I couldn't make myself tell him I got the shot; I feel like I've betrayed him.

I received my very first Concerned Parent letter—through e-mail, even! The one annotation is mine, the rest is hers.

To: ProfRuiz@wordsworth.edu
From: DebFoyle@dyne.com
Subject: Morbid Articles

Dear Professor Ruiz:

Hello. Let me introduce myself: my son Walter is taking your literature course. It's been hard to see him off to school as a freshman. He is very intelligent, and, well, he is the first one in our family to go to college. Paying for his education takes some sacrifice on our part. I feel a little out of my depth writing to you about this, since I know college is different, but I'm sincere and honest and I trust I can write to you. Walter has a chance at something his parents didn't have and I'm really worried it might go wrong. I was a member of the PTA and accustomed to be personally involved in his education. So I took it upon myself to read the books assigned for the course. I already feel educated myself by reading them (some I only looked through, to be honest) but what I read frightened me.

First I am sorry to see that you have demanded
of the students that they buy books on paper and
not on computer. Wasting good paper like that
when they could just the same read them on-screen.
The money we have spent on his equipment makes
it all the more upsetting. Could you consider using
electronic books in the future? His other classes use
them. But that is not the reason I am writing to you.

I am afraid that the morbid nature of the books
moves me to give you my opinion. The course seems
to be almost obsessive on death. If there isn't somebody dying, somebody's already dead! It is almost
funny, but I can't laugh. You understand, Walter is
young and sensitive, he gets that from me. I am
afraid they might influence him. I feel Walter is a
very sensitive child and we must protect him from
unnecessary concern. The world is a hard place,
and I do not want him to face it under such worries.
Life has been hard on me, I don't apologize for it,
but it has. I do not know you, I don't know how
your life has been, and why you would choose these
books. But I am really frightened by the thought
that something might happen to Walter, who has a
real chance of not having to make do month in
month out. I want the best for him. Wouldn't you?
I'm sorry, maybe I am just going crazy over here. I
really miss him. Please be good to my child.

I was particularly frightened by the homosexual
themes in some of the articles [Mrs. Foyle is referring
to "Death in Venice," dammit . . . and *Pale Fire,*
alas.-SR]. They are obviously presented in a way
that makes them futile and sad. I don't know how
homosexual's lives are, even though we respect their
right to be as they are Americans too, but are they so
unhappy? They can marry now. My sister is a nurse

and she tells me about how really nice they are. It's
sad enough to hear them die. And I stayed up awake
one whole night, frightened, thinking what if Walter
was homosexual? And I would not want that life
for him, especially if it is as sad as those books say.
That's why I want everything mean and ugly and
painful out of his life. I want things to be simple and
clean and good and easy to understand. And this is
getting too complicated for me. I am only his mother,
and I guess I can't do everything.

I keep thinking the morbid nature of the books
might be wrong for him. Maybe had I gone to college and read those books I wouldn't have made the
mistakes I have made. . . . My son sent me a copy of
a recent test of his. I am glad he had a B+ so he must
not be ignoring his studies. The question in the test
about art equals beauty plus pity, I don't understand, especially in the face of all this death.

Thanks for your time. Please ignore this letter
if you think I am wasting your time.

Question: Books have happy endings, too, don't
they?

So do faggots, ma'am. With God as my witness, so do faggots too!

To: DebFoyle@dyne.com
From: ProfRuiz@wordsworth.edu
Re: Morbid Articles

Dear Mrs. Foyle:

.   No, you are not wasting my time. It's nice to
hear someone care for their children. Thank you for
your concerned note.

Walter is quite definitely an intelligent young
man. I certainly do not want to drive him to suicide,

if that's what you're wondering about. He's doing fine. If he showed up drunk, stoned, or unprepared, I would have noticed—though, as far as I am concerned, it's up to the student to take the course seriously or not. I just flunk them if they don't. What I have noticed about Walter is that he's becoming more vocal in class discussions. He shows real character as a reader. His attention to the work being discussed is becoming keener, and the semester is only starting. I can forecast an improvement on his test grades given his growth in class. You should feel no worry, at least regarding what is within my purview as his professor.

It's a real pleasure to watch someone bloom in front of you. That's why I teach.

On the point of using books on paper, I'll tell you right off the bat that I'll continue to demand paper books until the university's administration licenses an e-book reader that makes it possible to make annotations like "Oh, that's just like me!" or "Right on!" or "ha, ha" or "Metaphor" or "Irony" on the margins of the screen. Scribbles make for easy browsing when one looks for a scene or sentence that's particularly intriguing. My books are full of such jottings.

Unfortunately, the powers that be signed a contract with the corporation that offered them the best deal but not the best product. The e-book reader that the students get for free has a strange habit of automatically misreading/mistranscribing my scribbles—they come out as "Arena," "Sinead ducky," and "This book is so guy!"—and you can't do a keyword search that includes your annotations. It's really annoying and, I'm sorry, that's just not acceptable. I could ask my students (and you, the parents) to spend money on a less institutionalized, higher quality electronic bookpad, but I'd have to go through an outside distributor for it. The institution here doesn't have a structure to order and sell other hardware (I suspect that's part of the agreement that gives us access to the "free" reader), but they do have a structure to order and sell books (I imagine the contractor doesn't see it as "competing technology"). So the choice has been made for me.

Sorry if I come off as kind of reactionary and insensitive. I am not afraid of technology. If I were, I'd be terrified of a lot of things I need to do to get along with people.

On morbidity and beauty:

Art is beauty plus pity because beauty never lasts. Because things are always changing, the world is always ending, beauty's always dying. What makes it so precious is what makes it so unstable and provisional. So the beautiful makes us feel sad. And if we really care about life, sadness is never too far behind. And so is joy, because, somewhere on the horizon, there is some new beauty waiting to be discovered, some strange mutation that will never be duplicated or equaled.

And if you can live with that every day and still feel the swoon of beauty in the face of all that dying, boy, I'd say you are some kind of grown-up.

I am working on this, and so are most of the students I hope to encourage on this path.

Ask Walter what he thinks of the class. I would think he does—

The phone rang. My husband.

"Sweetie," he said, "you doing anything tonight?"

"Nothing," I said, "just going over lecture notes."

"When are you coming home?"

"You can set a clock to my comings and goings, Charlie."

"I know. I was wondering if you were up for flatware tonight."

Two weeks since my shot, and, well, Charlie doesn't wait too long for a booty call.

"Dirty thoughts, eh?" I said.

"Yeah," he said. "Don't shoot your wad, eh?"

Charlie and I can be very Canadian about sex.

As I hung up, I thought: Do I love him because he's going to die? Do I hate myself because I cannot? Am I being just a tad grandiose?

I didn't finish the letter, but I saved it to finish later.

The two weeks during which the C3PO immuno-expressant corps began to take over my body went pretty much without incident. Other than Charlie being particularly cuddly and patient with me. It was infuriating. The first signs of dementia settling in. I don't know, maybe the feeling that he had something to support me about made him feel that much closer to me, made him feel useful. And, of course, I made a show of trusting him right and left.

The other day, I let him take me out to dinner and the movies. He got the popcorn. I held our seats, frightened that he would faint or something while standing in line. I was so grateful when he came back, even if he forgot the Good & Plenty. But I'm not supposed to be courted, I'm not supposed to have problems, he's the one who's sick. He wasn't very mopey to begin with, but now he's positively bursting into song at the onset of some emotion—or a bowel movement.

Other than that, my health is more or less the same. I

would hope to mutate into some monster, something more frightening, like a dung beetle. At least I'd have an excuse to leave him. All that's changed is that I'm sleeping better. And I wake up with this furry guy curled up against me, this guy who's growing chubbier all the time.

Charlie's too good for me. I'm going to have to leave him. After all we've gone through, he's still too good for me, and I don't deserve him. Living with him is such excruciating torture nowadays, knowing he's going to kick the bucket, and him having nothing but sweetness for me. Me, who's probably going to get tenure. I just feel so . . . I feel so *wrong*.

So I'm going to have some unprotected sex with him just to please him, and then I'll find some way of moving near campus in a jiff. That's my parting gift: the contamination of my precious bodily fluids. Then: exile.

I can't stand this anymore. I'm burning my candle at both ends, and I forget how the rest of this quote goes.

I hope Charlie will understand.

I get home to find Charlie pouring white sauce over cannelloni stuffed with some high-cholesterol paté and ground beef. His only greeting is a lifted eyebrow and a stroke of his goatee. I drop my briefcase on a kitchen chair.

"How are you feeling?" I ask.

"Abominable," he says.

There are candles on the table, flowers in a vase as if they were arranged by Robert Mapplethorpe, and, displayed where I cannot help but notice it, a can of Crisco.

"I've been slaving over the stove all day," he says. "Dinner will be ready in half an hour."

It's so weird to have Charlie take care of me. It's so wrong. He's the one who has to be taken care of, not me.

"This takes my breath away," I say, "and quite possibly

my appetite, too. You can't be spending your energy like this. What a spread you've put out for me."

"In a manner of speaking," he says, cocking his butt.

Let me change the subject. "No, I'm serious. You shouldn't be overextending yourself."

"Oh, Camilla and Sue helped out. And I paced myself. I've been working on this all week, really. No need for you to feel guilty."

"It's a sin."

"Well, ain't it just!" Charlie licks a speck of sauce off his wrist. "Help me toss the salad? Or shall I toss myself—that is, shall I toss the salad?."

"Let me overcompensate on the salad," I groaned.

So out comes the cutting board and the cucumber. The cuke I slice so thin the slices should melt in his mouth. After hubby puts the pan of pasta in the oven, he sits down to watch me slice.

I am so nervous I slice my middle finger.

"F-f-fuck!"

"Let me have a look," Charlie says.

"Oh, all right," I say, and give him the bird.

And then he takes my cut finger in his hand.

And he ever so slowly kisses it, and pops it in his mouth, and sucks it.

Dinner burns in the oven. Spoons, forks, and knives remain untouched on the table, all in their correct order and placement.

The amazing thing is, one can love something that can die. The irrational thing. That is the enchantment. That one could love a losing proposition, that one can love the transitory, and still remain in the moment, in the moment before that beauty passes away.

And if this is turning into a world where mystery and pain are eliminated to make for a——

Let me not overinterpret this.

I would hope that my bionic ImmunoHelpers have traveled into him through the spit in my kisses, and through other methods of injection—methods that I will not reveal in order to remain within the bounds of good taste. And if my attemps at sharing my love and my health fail to extend his life, or make mine uncomfortable . . . well, fuck it.

At least I gave it a shot.

Public Displays of Affection

i.

Dean and Mark had one highly disastrous blind date brokered by the married-couple-to-be. The Shakespeare in the Park show of *Much Ado About Nothing* was rained out, the queues at the restaurants were murderously long, and neither of them knew how to broach the subject of why this date was a bad idea and why they should just stop pretending they wanted to be with each other and head their separate ways. But the existential gulf between them had not been caused by rain or queues or Shakespeare but by a rather awkward, disappointed hello.

That they managed for the two years since the blind date from hell not to spoil everyone's party with slow burns and cutting words was a credit to their social skills. It was well-known to their acquaintances that while they were not the best of friends, they could be expected to behave around each other like gentlemen, if not to actually ignore each other—which is what they appeared to do. Socially, they became familiar to each other, each like a piece of ugly furniture that litters a room but helps define it.

Mark was friends with Julian, the groom, who used to be in his band and was now a record company executive; Dean, of Mary, the bride, who was his last girlfriend and now a comedy writer. The engaged couple were to have their religious and familial ceremony in the bride's hometown. In order to accommodate their New York City friends, their close circle in showbiz and the arts, they held the civil formality in Manhattan and made it the occasion for a small soirée with the goal of increased good times and hey nonny nonny.

As is true with most socially sanctioned events, like seasonal festivals, cultural pride events, and otherwise irrelevant milestones, a smidgen of emotional weight crept in, unannounced, displacing the event's function as an excuse to party, get drunk, and maybe fornicate. There were other interesting people at the event, people worth noting, but, excluding the newlyweds, Dean and Mark had something of an issue with the idea of a wedding ceremony and the people in it. It was a *wedding*—an affair that neither Mark nor Dean could look forward to. It was the wedding of two of their best friends. Life would significantly change. That the word *love* came to mind when thinking about them—God, they couldn't imagine a life without Mary and Julian—made the event resonate.

Ink was put on paper. Stamps and permits accepted. Applause. Handshakes and kisses and hugs. Guess who wouldn't shake hands, hug, or kiss each other.

ii.

Mary and Julian signed their papers in a typical hall of justice, with unflattering overhead office lighting and cheap veneer paneling that alluded to some kind of wood, shabby and boring enough to be a space where everyone was equally uncomfortable under the eyes of the law. Rooms like this exuded an air of official indifference: architecture well-suited to anything from minor arraignments to depositions or small-claims cases. The seal of the State of New York looked peremptory, an icon no one kissed; the audience benches, humbled, knew their place.

The twenty or so revelers buzzed around the newly government-sanctioned couple. Mark had quietly slipped into the room while the ceremony began and stood in a corner of the chamber to observe as a member of the jury; it was over before he had a chance to lean against the wall. He slowly made his way through the crowd toward the couple, thinking: This is never going to happen to me. All the while waving quietly to whoever recognized his presence on his way to Mary and Julian.

Mark thought he wasn't a dramatic sort. He prided himself on his stoic nature in the face of fate. A slight feeling of abandonment crept in. As if he were being left behind. He put on his best face—reserved, yet friendly—and yet couldn't help noticing how other people did not seem anxious about congratulating the couple, as if there were no extraordinary risk in getting married. Perhaps, Mark thought, he didn't have the temperament for either sentiment or marriage. Everyone seemed to wear their emotions more comfortably than he did, to burst forward to be noticed, while he was more deliberate. He couldn't tell jokes well. Saying that he was happy for the couple would be just as difficult. There was something to expressing things spontaneously, without considering the consequences of such a revelation, that he couldn't trust.

But he had to.

iii.

Dean practically burst out with the champagne bottle for Mary and Julian as soon as the justice of the peace uttered the last word. He came forward as if it were his party. And it sort of was: Dean had introduced the couple to each other as they had introduced him to Mark, and he was hosting the affair. He'd gotten there early with a heavy cooler full of ice and chilled bottles of champagne and plastic fluted glasses, so heavy he could hardly carry it by himself, and greeted everyone as they came in. Later, in his apartment, the guests would eat, drink, and be merry while the couple drove off to Oradell, New Jersey, for the religious ring-swapping. Dean went around the room exchanging amiable chitchat—even with the judge, whom he asked, "Do you think you could marry me to a guy?"—handing everyone glasses and filling them with champagne.

Dean, rather than be sidelined by a celebration of heterosexual franchise, would make it his occasion as well. He enjoyed throwing parties for people anyway, even heterosexuals. He served everyone quickly and gracefully, working his way around the room as the couple were being congratulated for their decision to make it official, separate tax forms notwithstanding. He felt pleasure at seeing others enjoy themselves, and it was the chance to provide and behold pleasure that made his life worth living.

Dean had gotten enough plastic champagne flutes and enough champagne for the invited and accounted for. Few glasses were left. He picked two off the table and sought anyone who was left unchampered. It would be strange for him to fill his glass alone; people came in twos that evening: Penny and Jim, Frank and Laurie, and so on and so forth. Dean and. . . ? Funny how that would hit him now. It spoiled the fun. He hadn't thought of inviting anyone. He'd be too busy playing host to really pay attention to anyone, anyway. Besides, he'd have to be dating someone to have someone to bring.

A quick look at the crowd revealed a lone, lanky man approaching the couple with his hands in his pockets. It was Mark. Mark with that quiet, angry face, who always seemed to not like him, to disapprove of him silently. Why Mark was kept hanging around in spite of his obvious indifference to the world was a mystery to Dean. Well, Mary kept telling him that he was shy, but Dean would not suffer that.

He approached Mark for the sake of the couple.

"Here," Dean said curtly, offering him a glass. "Join the party."

iv.

Just when Mark was going to approach the lucky two, the little man with the big ego, who could almost not be ignored, stopped him in his tracks with a glass of champagne.

"Isn't it against the law to drink in courtrooms?" Mark asked, and was about to turn again to Mary and Julian.

"Shush . . ." Dean whispered, leaning closer to Mark.

In Mark's experience, Dean had a habit of taking everything personally. One of those smart, charming, attractive men who think the world revolves around them. That he bullied him for proof of his charm anytime they interacted was something Mark resented as quickly as he noticed Dean's eyes. They were rather beautifully blue.

"All right," Mark said. "I'll have one."

"Good," Dean said.

"Excuse me, I must talk with Julian and Mary," Mark said. Mark turned to Julian and Mary, who were talking and laughing with another couple, and stopped to consider his approach.

"Funny how Julian and Mary have become a single noun," Dean said a little sadly perhaps. "Julianandmary. Maryandjulian."

Why was Dean talking to him all of a sudden? Mark thought Dean hated him.

The little man stood in front of him and lifted his glass as if he were toasting Mark.

v.

"Yes," Mark said, and lifted the glass as well, and drank.

Were those the corners of his mouth turning upwards?

Dean thought. "I . . . I am really happy for them," Dean said. "God, that's sounds weird, I am happy *because* of them."

The lanky, dry-tempered man stopped looking back and forth between him and the couple as if he'd been seeking somewhere to escape.

"Why 'because'?" Mark asked.

Dean was shocked that Mark was actually listening. "Well . . . it's nice to see one's friends be happy and have what everyone seems to want."

There was a strange sense of satisfaction in the fact that Mark finally appeared to react to him and not to voices from outer space.

"Does everyone want to be married?" Mark asked.

"Apparently," Dean said. "Or at least everyone wants the world to know that they're in love. They want to be in love in public. Or they want to be acknowledged publicly for it."

"I see," Mark said.

"That's assuming they are marrying for love. Which they are, of course. . . ."

Dean fought the idea that he had been misunderstanding Mark all this time. Maybe he had misinterpreted his reticence as a kind of casual contempt.

"I think they are," Mark said.

vi.

"Weddings . . . funny things, aren't they?" Dean said. "By the way, did you . . . did you ever catch that play?"

"Which one?" Mark asked.

"The one . . . the one we missed. You know, that time. *Much Ado.*"

"I didn't."

"Why not? It was *fabulous.*"

"I don't go to the theater alone."

"I do," Dean said. "I do it often. . . . I caught the next performance. I was wondering . . . you are familiar with Willie the Shakes?"

"Yes."

"I've been thinking, and I must be weird to think of this . . . don't you ever wonder if the leads who don't get married off in the comedies are . . . are gay? It's like they are singled out at the end."

"They're not really part of the story."

"But they've got the best lines! I mean, who *really* cares about the *ingenues*?"

"They observe and comment. They don't get involved."

"But that's not *fair*!" Dean said.

"You really like Shakespeare," Mark said.

"Oh, anyway, I'm only a *dilettante*. I never remember characters' names. The duke or prince or whatever does not get married at the end of *Much Ado*."

"He didn't. You're right."

"It sort of bugged me. I don't know why."

"Should it bother you that he doesn't get married?"

"Within reason," Dean said.

"Good answer," Mark said.

vii.

Mark sipped from the glass of champagne to fill his silence. There was not much he could say. Evidently, all that Dean wanted was to be noticed. Not like hogging a stage; more like asking to be said hello to in spite of there being no feelings between them. Very little to ask for. That Dean attempted to make small talk in the face of Mark's indifference in the past, Mark found curious and engaging. Dean must think well of him regardless, Mark thought. Mark felt guilty at the thought of his insensitivity.

"Oh, pray not let me disturb you," Dean said, waving

him off toward Julian and Mary. "Go ahead, kiss them for me. . . . I've got to leave this place as I found it—not that I put up streamers or anything. . . . Looks like everyone's about to head to my apartment! Gotta run!"

"Would you like to come with me?" Mark said. "To say hello to Mary and Julian?"

Mark stood there, motionless, trying hard not to show that he would really like Dean to come along with him.

A little shy smile, *that,* he couldn't hold back.

viii.

Dean had a face that announced his every feeling like a pinball machine. Mark had lighted it up.

"Why . . . of course, yes!" Dean said. "If it's not an imposition. . . ."

"It's not," Mark said.

Why, Dean thought, he is a shy one, really! How funny and delightful it was to be surprised.

"Thank you," Mark said.

"For what?"

"For the glass of champagne," he said. "And the Shakespeare."

Mark blushed. And tried to sip from an empty glass of champagne.

"Let me take that from you," Dean said.

"Let's talk to them first. . . ."

"Absolutely!" Dean said.

Like two knights drawing near the king and queen to show their fealty, they approached the newlyweds. The newlyweds, in turn, took each other's hand as if a miracle had occurred, and burst into giddy laughter.

ix.

As the members of the wedding party slowly left the room to congregate at Dean's doorstep, the couples huddled.

"Conga rats, sweetie," Dean said to Mary, before hugging and kissing her.

"Good job," said Mark to Julian, their handshake turning into a hearty hug.

"You're with Mark!" Mary whispered to Dean.

"Got lucky?" Julian whispered to Mark.

"Uh . . . no," Mark said.

"Now don't get any ideas," Dean said.

They switched partners and hugged.

"Go for it," Julian whispered to Dean.

"Dean really likes you," Mary whispered to Mark.

Neither gay man had a response to this.

They unhuddled and stood in front of each other.

Julian and Mary glanced at each other and started giggling.

Dean interpreted the giggle as another expression of their being so caught up in each other they couldn't stand not being delirious. Mark took it as the private joke that couples always seemed to share. The ambient noise in the room considerably decreased as the larger party disassembled and withdrew stage left.

"Oh, shit," Dean said. "I'm gonna be late! Gotta run. See ya in a bit." He nodded to all three and ran off to pick up the bottles and glasses.

"Thanks for inviting me," Mark said.

"Dean looks like he's all caught up with no one to help him," Mary said.

"Yeah!" Julian said, turning to Mark. "Did you know that Dean's been helping us out with this? He could use a hand."

"Really?"

Julian slapped Mark's shoulder. "Wake up, guy!"

"Should I help?" Mark asked.

"I think Dean would appreciate it," Mary added.

"All right." Mark said.

"See you at the party," Mary said.

Through the door that many a couple had entered as two and left as one under the law, Dean stood at a folding table provided for his use and quickly stuffed empties and glasses in a plastic bag. Mary and Julian crossed arms around each other's backs while watching Mark make a considered approach with an empty glass that Dean had missed, a glass that had perched precariously on top of a knobbly radiator, and held it with his own in one elegant hand.

Dean caught Mark approaching him with two glasses and smiled as Mark dropped them neatly into the thick gray bag Dean held open for him like welcoming arms.

"Thank you," Dean said. "Uh . . . I think that's it for the glasses. . . ."

Dean stuffed the trash bag inside the ice-filled cooler and closed it. "Do you want to share a taxi?" Mark asked.

"Sure," Dean said. "We better hurry."

"They can wait," Mark said.

"Let us go then, you and I," Dean said.

The door closed behind Mark and Dean silently as they left the room. They carried the portable cooler between them by its handles. It took them about five minutes to flag a taxi. When they arrived at Dean's apartment building, they found most of the wedding party waiting calmly by the front door.

§

Rog & Venus Become an Item

Rog had become a celebrity. His large, bloody placenta and umbilical cord never failed to arouse interest and attention at parties. It was his ticket to notoriety, a conversation piece that grew out of his own gut: folds of red tissue like a slab of beef, a capillary mass covered with semitransparent tissue, at one end extended to an umbilical cord and connected to his body, and at the other, folded into lips that when opened revealed bean-shaped suckers not unlike those of a squid. His sinuous, coiled link was covered with a soft, translucent skin, two arteries and one vein visible within it. It smelled like rust and blood. He carried it inside a briefcase. On more casual occasions he would carry it in a hip bag slung low on his waist like a gun holster. It was more comfortable to pack it and carry it along than to let it hang out and bleed on the floor. It would also tug hard on him if he threw it over his shoulder.

The umbilical cord ran outside through a notch by the case handle, then right up under his coat, through his shirt and into his tummy. On request, when things started to let down during the course of the evening's entertainment, he would open the briefcase, pull out and open the Ziploc bag where he kept the mass most of the time, spread it on his lap or on a table, secrete amniotic fluids, and wiggle it for his audience.

Such talents were rare, but not unknown. The official word on him chalked up his placenta to his relatively exotic Latino heritage. But the normally jaded public was impressed, if not by its novelty, by the placenta itself. People would look at the flow of the red and blue blood within it. It was a psychedelic experience, quite absorbing. Still, not everybody was pleased with it. A small but influential magazine had this to say about his mixed-media work, and, by association, his placenta:

"In essence, it is a curiosity whose appeal is limited and will be short-lived. Intentionally artless bile vehemently spit upon the face of the observer like a bursting boil, it is, in effect, a glorified lava lamp: inconsequential and, at best, cute."

But then, that's what it said about most everything.

Rog was painfully aware of this and worked hard on extending his fifteen minutes. He kept his placenta scrupulously clean and had it trimmed frequently, keeping it alive but not letting it grow to such a size that it would suck the blood that would normally go to other parts of his body. For Rog, any inconvenience it might cause was a burden he had to carry. Any risk that the placenta entailed was a chance he had to take.

So Rog hung on to the placenta and to the idea that he had become famous despite himself. He had gone through school without a sense of achievement: while standing in line to place his request for a B.F.A. degree at the registrar's office, he realized that he had learned very little and matured even less, saddled with a gift of dubious value. At school, reclusive and bashful, he stuffed the Ziploc bag down his pants or taped it to his back, trying not to call attention to it. "That's not his dick hanging down the side of his pants, dear," said one of Rog's teachers to an inquisitive fellow student at the opening night of his graduate show, when his umbilical cord had shifted from under his shirt and loosened inside his trousers. Rog quickly put his hands inside his pants and nervously pulled out the placenta. He looked around in embarrassment for a rest room when a couple, wishing to congratulate him on his fingerpaint and Colorform collages, stopped him before the men's room door.

"Hi," said Rog, holding his appendage against his lap. The couple, two patrons of the arts, looked at it with astonishment.

"What's that?" the man asked, pointing.

"A placenta," Rog said under his breath.

"Why . . . ," said the woman, widening her eyes, "it's beautiful!"

"Yes," her husband said, nodding enthusiastically. "Yes."

Rog couldn't believe how their faces seemed to light up, not just with curiosity and amazement, but with delight and wonder, at the sight of his afterbirth. Soon a small crowd formed around him to contemplate it and smile gratefully, and Rog suddenly felt pretty good about himself.

He ended up making his first sale that night to the couple, who took home an Amish-style chair sculpted out of Play-Doh.

After this revelation, his problem wasn't anything that a good haircut and an Armani suit couldn't fix.

He got a day job at a gallery. People there invariably asked him what was inside the briefcase and then he showed them. With such an instantly recognizable trademark, it didn't take long for him to hook up to the social network, and he didn't need a day job. Recently, his work had been featured in the window of the gallery where he used to work.

Still, though his career was coming along nicely, he despaired. He thought people liked him, not for who he was, but because of his placenta. He thought that he didn't deserve to be loved.

At a party at a Long Island mansion, celebrating the opening of a new gallery, Rog was standing in line for the buffet table. He was looking forward to helping himself to the beautifully laid out spread when he carelessly bumped into a stunningly beautiful woman standing in line before him.

"Sorry," Rog said as she turned to him.

"Hi," said the young woman, who had short, straight, jet black hair as shiny as polyester, a square face, pale skin, big, red, sexy lips and mouth. She wore clothes that brought to mind a mourning peasant: a shawl, a black blouse like a priest's, a long, fluffy, black skirt, black flats, a few crosses hanging between her breasts.

"Hello," Rog said. She looked with concern at his briefcase and the twisting cord that came out of it and ran up under his jacket.

"I just can't let go of this," he said, and he shrugged and smiled.

"Oh, I'm sorry, I didn't mean to stare," she said.

"It's OK." Rog grabbed a plate with his free hand. She went to the clam bar and waited politely for the line to move on. He trailed behind her, wondering about the impression he'd made. Trying to think of something charming to say about the fête, he set himself the difficult task of serving himself while holding onto both plate and placenta.

After an abortive effort, in which he dropped the briefcase, yanking the length of his cord with an effect similar to having his internal organs sucked out by an industrial vacuum cleaner, the mourning peasant approached him.

"Are you all right?" she asked.

"I'm fine," he said, doubled up on himself, his arms wrapped around the briefcase, holding it against his chest.

He staggered off aimlessly and ended up on a couch in a small, secluded alcove to lick his wounds. He stared at the floor, trying not to think, not to sink into self-pity, just to take the pain, shut up, and go on.

She'd followed him to the room. "Feeling better?" she asked with a coy, affected voice.

Rog looked up and saw her standing before him.

"A little."

"Look, can I get you something? I can't stand to watch you there looking like a helpless puppy. Humor me, at least."

Rog looked at her and couldn't tell if he should be in pain or in love, or both.

"Being a helpless puppy myself," she said, speaking in a self-mockingly heroic tone, "I can't help but rescue you." She giggled nervously. "Please let me help you."

Rog laughed, charmed, even though it hurt him.

"Let me get you something from the table," she said.

She went away without waiting for his answer. She brought him clams, some slices of lemon, and a glass of champagne. She sat down.

"Thank you very much," Rog said.

"It's nothing, really."

"Nothing for yourself?"

"I'm not really hungry. This apple will do."

"I hope you forgive me, but eating clams can be very embarrassing."

"Don't worry. I know bivalves inside out. Stop being so apologetic."

"I'm sorry," he said with a goofy smile.

"Come on!" she said and playfuly slapped his arm. She bit the apple and the apple's skin cut the gums between her front teeth.

"Are you a biologist?" he said as he split a clam apart.

She bit again and the blood in her saliva colored the pulp pink.

"Not yet. Working on it, though. Is that a dialysis unit there?"

"Where?"

"In your briefcase."

"Oh . . . no."

"Then, what is it?"

"I'll show you later." He slurped in the glossy, gummy substance.

"A cousin of mine has to be connected to one, and he straps it over his back like scuba gear. Like my stepdad, he's had a colostomy done and has a tube coming out of his intestine into a bag taped to his back."

"Colostomy?"

"He had colon and rectal cancer, and they cut it out before it spread everywhere else and attached what was left to the tube. Now he shits into a bag. Anyway, what I meant is that he was hooked up into something himself."

"Oh," Rog said, and nodded.

"He's taking it well. He's only got a couple of years left, you know, but he really doesn't mind. He's going to have himself frozen, like Walt Disney. Wow, you really slurped up those clams."

"I'm sort of eating for two."

"Huh?" she asked.

"Never mind," Rog said. "Want to see what's in the briefcase?"

"Sure."

He put his plate on a side table and opened the briefcase.

"That's a placenta," she said.

He opened the Ziploc, pulled it out, and laid it on the table in front of her. "Yes. Do you like it?"

"Oh, it's kind of weird-looking, in a way," she said. "Like the ones that came with our fetal pigs, only bigger. And it's red, not like theirs, they're kind of sickly blue, but that's because they're preserved, and they stink."

"Mine doesn't stink, huh?" Rog said, his smile curling playfully as he separated the folds in his lump of meat to show her its suckers.

"Can I touch them?"

"Feel free," he said. She touched a suction cup and it seemed to suck her finger, ever so slightly.

"That feels so eerie," she said. She ran her fingers over the glossy membrane. Rog felt his blood quicken. He gazed at her intensely. He felt as if he were going to burn right through her.

Suddenly, she pulled away from him. Rog was stunned by the abrupt withdrawal of her touch.

"Oh, I'm sorry . . . ," she said as she grasped her hand as if trying to assure herself that it was still there.

"It's all right. It's perfectly all right. Don't apologize."

After an awkward silence and an exchange of dazed smiles, he started to pack his placenta away.

"How long have you had your placenta?" she asked.

"Ever since I can remember," Rog said.

She blushed and laughed, covering her mouth with her hands as if trying to prevent more words from coming out of it. "I know, I know, stupid question . . . ," She threw her head back, her mouth wide open, her lips full, her neck stretched out and milky white. The image became fixed in his mind, like a snapshot.

"Keep the questions coming," he said. "I'd love to answer them."

"Let's go get some drugs," she said.

They spent the rest of the night talking about art, death, shit, and other secretions.

A week later they did lunch.

A week after that he took her to his studio and showed her what he was working on. He was building a two-to-one scale refrigerator to go with several mock outsider art pieces portraying various scenes of domestic horror in a psychotic, childlike manner, which he planned to stick on the fridge with magnets. Later that same day, she took him to the lab where she did her practical biological experiments. He watched her cut up various developing chick embryo cell layers into parts and implant them into a whole, shell-bound egg white in order to incubate and develop disembodied eyes, muscles, skin, etcetera.

As their courtship went on, they started to send each other silly and useless gifts, like beautifully gift-wrapped boxes of air, olive green toasters, framed Velvis and flamenco dancer portraits, plastic bonsai trees, dead pigeons, and snot. For Halloween, Rog dressed himself as Louis Pasteur and brought a stuffed toy, Purulent Penelope, his favorite cow and concubine, as his date. She dressed up as Madame Curie, her skin covered with radioactive green, glowing latex sores.

They began getting deeply involved in each other's activities. Rog drew some photo-realistic anatomical renderings that were going to be used as guides by students, scientific drawings that he had volunteered to produce for her school. She posed for a photograph in which she lay dressed in a wedding gown on a pile of intestines strewn out on the floor of her lab, which he later painted and featured in his first commercial illustration work, the cover of Gross National Product's *Incontinence* album. Rog let his hair grow long and soon had a ponytail at the back of his head, tied with a strip of black lace. Venus started to wear red dresses often.

Rog was invited to be guest specimen for the day in an embryology class that Venus was taking. In the hall outside the classroom, in an atmosphere redolent of ether and preservatives, Venus seemed strangely distant.

"So, what are you doing tonight," Rog asked her, caressing the back of her neck.

"I don't know," she said, pulling away from him.

"We can go up to my place," Rog said. "I can make you an omelette or something."

"Let's just . . . ," she said and suddenly held onto her bosom, angry. ". . . I just don't feel . . ."

"What's wrong," he asked her. "Did I do something?"

"No, it's got nothing to do with you," she barked at him.

"Well, can I help?"

"Don't worry about me," she said and shrugged him off. "Look, I'll write you a letter, OK?" She stormed into the classroom. Is it her period? Rog asked himself. Is she pregnant? He got really scared all of a sudden. He didn't quite understand these kinds of things.

He walked into the room. As the students congregated and took their seats, Rog pulled out his placenta to place on the examination table. As he spread it open, he noticed that it was unusually active, gurgling and undulating. He felt his pulse go up and his breath quicken. Rog looked up to Venus, who was sitting in the back of the room, and he shuddered. She shuffled in her seat, gritted her teeth, and wrapped her arms tightly around herself. She avoided his gaze. Rog loosened his tie. She stood up and ran out crying.

Rog grabbed his placenta as it was and ran out after her.

"Venus!" he shouted as he ran up to her and cornered her at the end of the corridor, blocking the doorway with his body, staring her down.

"Let me go, let me go," she said, turning back from him. As she pulled away, he noticed that his placenta was stretching and contracting in his sweaty hands.

She ran into the ladies' room nearby. Rog stood by the door, sporting a raging hard-on, not knowing quite what to do.

After a while, Rog calmed down, wiped his brow, and went back to the classroom, hoping that Venus would feel better soon and show up for the lecture.

He didn't see or hear from her until she wrote him a note a week later.

Rog:

    This is kind of difficult for me to say. . . . I
don't know, I just want to show you that I'm not
a psycho. . . . I hope that you don't mind us not seeing each other for a while. I need to breathe. I need
my space, for a little while. It's not forever, you
know, and . . . well, who knows? Venus.

Rog didn't take long to answer.

Venus:

    I'll let you breathe. I'll be your space, I'll be your
atmosphere. It may not be forever, but it might be
too long already. . . . Let's take a risk. Let's go shopping. We'll take it slow. Love, Rogelio.

    She soon appeared at his doorstep with a shopping list.
They went to a record store, Rog's favorite. They knew
him there. He didn't have to leave his hip bag at the front
counter and didn't need to explain to them why it was
physically impossible to do so. Rog's favorite store marked
all its record bins as Music in order to avoid making any
unfair classifications and to keep its customers from trying
something different. Venus favored goth rock and Rog
liked techno pop, both of which had a distinct *Life is bor-
ing/People are boring/Jesus is boring/The weather is bor-
ing/I'm so depressed/I wanna die/Ooh, baby, baby/I love
you* lyric to them.

    "Maybe we can live with each other," she said as they
were on their way out of the store, shopping bags in hand.
He darted a look at her sweetly calm countenance, raised
his eyebrows.

    "Ah . . . after you," he said, moving forward to open the
door for her.

    "No," she said, dropping her bags, staying put. "After
you."

"Are you making this an issue?" he asked, holding the heavy door wide open.

"Yeah," she said, crossing her arms defiantly over her chest. "I've read *The Second Sex*. I know what it is to be a woman."

"Can't argue with that," he said, dropping his shopping bags on the floor, a lanky arm holding the door firmly, his body swinging over to block the exit, the hip bag pressing against the frame. He smiled slyly, crossed his legs, the steel tip of his shoe dropping on the floor with a click.

"I said, maybe we can live with each other," Venus said, standing proudly.

He held his stance before her proposition and ceremoniously let go of the door. The door's spring mechanism immediately tried to slam it shut. Instead, it slammed on the placenta, which was stuck between door and frame, and cut their argument short.

"Maybe," he muttered, feeling his knees give under him.

He felt her catching him before he fell. He walked sluggishly toward safety with her support. Before long he found himself sitting down on a sofa in the record store's unoccupied ladies' room.

"You've . . . got . . . all the . . . shopping . . . bags?" he asked, breathless, his head swimming, his face contorted and pale.

"Who gives a fuck about the shopping bags," she said, unzipping the hip bag, tenderly drawing out the placenta.

She pulled it out of the bag and put it on her lap. It was bloodier than usual, and some blood spilled onto her beautiful red dress. She inspected it with tentative hands and found one of its edges swollen and purple, bleeding and pulsing erratically. He stared point-blank at her intense eyes, which suddenly lit up even brighter. She pulled a lacy handkerchief from her purse in such a rush that all its contents spilled out, contacts and compacts and Tampax flying in all directions. She folded the handkerchief and began to swab the placenta carefully, cleaning it with a corner of cloth tucked between the tips of her fine fingers.

"Is it . . . a . . . wound?" Rog whispered, turning closer to her as he struggled to speak.

"No, it's a just a bruise," she said. "Bruises happen. Some things just can't be helped." Rog felt the inflamed purple capillaries coming down to a slow throb and saw the bloodshed stop under her care, under her concerned gaze, and realized that she really wasn't scared. And paroxysms of pain couldn't stop the desire that mounted in him.

"Let's set Christmas trees on fire," he said as he caught his breath. "Let's say ridiculously romantic things to each other. Let's not live in sin."

"What monster have I loosed upon the world?" she said, throwing her hands up in the air, waving the damp, red handkerchief, eyes swirling to the ceiling.

"Some things just can't be helped," he said.

Venus lay asleep on his bed later that day, half-draped with soft, fleecy sheets in the same way that kitschy French Academy painters would drape their sex objects. And it was proper. Her figure was full and well-rounded, just the way the French Academy had portrayed perfection. Rog agreed with their statement. He put his head on her tummy and kissed it. He kissed it again. He looked at her navel. She was an innie. It's a world of innies and outies, he thought. If humanity really were to be classified by the ways their little umbilical strips were knotted, folded, and tucked into their bellies, he would be an outcast. Again, he felt the pangs of insecurity. He didn't know why, but he felt as if he were misbegotten, born without a sense of belonging or wholeness. He wondered why such thoughts would impinge upon him as if God were speaking. After all, he'd made it. He was famous and he was in love. Life was good. Perhaps too good? He tried to give up on that idea. He did not have the time or the inclination for another irrational belief. He embraced her waist. She caressed his neck, still half-asleep. He turned around and pulled himself closer to her sweet neck and she ran her hand over him, her fingers combing through the hair on his chest.

He pulled his placenta closer to him and he opened the bag. The tender folds of capillaries and skin stirred, the suckers inside frothy and gurgling. He gently placed it open on her lap and spread her legs apart. . . .

Rog and Venus have since become an item, their fates inextricably linked. You can't see one without the other.

§

Up Close

I hold onto a giant, floating E. M. Forster with seven other people in period costume, wave as we walk down the avenue toward Times Square and then farther south to the docklands, and I pretend to be dour and love nature. I would have chosen Walt Whitman, but I had no choice. This year's theme is Modernist Queers. We guide inflatables in the shape of gay icons—Oscar Wilde, Gertrude Stein, Marcel Proust, Willa Cather, Colette. . . . The float ahead of us presents the *tableaux* of a mollyhouse, men dressed as women taunting and teasing both each other and the men dressed as men. A marching band follows us, playing some period song of same-sex love, sponsored by a condom enterprise. We have spared no detail, no expense. We have corporate sponsorship, media coverage. There will be a video for sale, which I'm going to buy. I'd like to see what they did for the twenties, with flappers and tuxedoed women in a washtub-gin setting. Serving in spectacles does not permit me to watch them (unless someone records them). Instead, I hold onto the role model, hoping it won't float away, hoping it won't float away with me. Perhaps this year the message will get through that we are not like everyone, that we are gods, that you must adore us, that you must want us, that you must fear us. We need to present a proud heritage. I've not yet decided whether I feel pride or vainglory: here we are, the best and the brightest, look who we are, look who we could be. If you had no one to watch from a distance, you'd have to look at yourself, and we'd have to look at ourselves. My headset walkie-talkie buzzes: someone has fainted from heatstroke on the corseted lesbian suffragette float.

Other People's Complications

Kip arrived at the studio to find Mark crying over the mixing board. Mark hunched over the console as though he'd been told to take a nap while everyone else completed a test he knew he'd failed. Kip stood by the door, his body angling forward as if waiting to be allowed into the room. Mark sobbed quietly, sighed.

"Listen . . . should I come back later?" Kip asked.

Mark finally noticed him, lifted his head from the crook of his arm.

"Just give me a moment," Mark said, sounding as if he'd lost his voice.

"All right, then."

Kip turned around and made his way out, wondering just how much time they could afford to lose that morning. For a fleeting moment, he wondered what had happened to break his friend's even temper, but Kip chose to ignore that thought. He really wasn't interested.

Kip bought the *Times* from a street vendor's booth. He bought a blended fruit juice and a bagel with a smear of cream cheese at a bagel shop busy with rude, harried morning traffic and mispelled signs for food items on sale. He tried to eat but he couldn't read. He wondered, when was the last time he'd seen Mark cry?

Mark got close to tears the night they drank themselves to incoherence to celebrate the fact that they'd been dumped by their label: their music had been seen as too different from traditional rock and roll to have any longevity in the marketplace. Music rags declared them New Wave one-hit wonders.

It was that feeling of being given up on, discarded, that hit them the hardest in their youth, and that disappointment still managed to trouble. Mark and Kip made a comeback as a production team, the kind of producer and engineer that knowing music critics mentioned by name. Their knob twiddling and session work maintained a level of innovation and polish that set them apart from mere competence. But they could still be discarded again, regardless. The possibility that they could have been dismissed again broke Kip's concentration. Mark and Kip's partnership was a pocket universe of security in a pretty awful industry. Knowing for certain that the world was not as beneficent as they wished it could be bonded them to each other. Studio talent could work for years and years if they were reliable and kept up with the technology and fashion. Maybe they'd been wrong. Had they been fired?

He spilled his orange-papaya juice on his paper; lifting the folds of newsprint off the table for a moment, he watched the liquid trickle lamely down the page. Better to let it soak up the spill; he threw it back down on the table.

Kip returned to the studio and found Mark on a splicing workstation on the far side of the booth, using a razor to cut out part of a drum sequence that might be usable. The sight brought Kip out of his panic.

Mark cleared his throat. "Don't worry, this is a copy. I'm going to make a tape loop," he said.

"For a moment there you had me thinking something had happened," Kip said.

"Work heals," Mark said.

Kip let that float in the air, then rolled a chair to the workstation and plopped himself down on it.

"So, we're all right then," he asked.

"*We're* all right," Mark said.

"So something did happen," Kip said.

"It's not really that interesting."

"You know I freak out when you don't tell me stuff. I start making shit up, and it makes me feel like you don't trust me."

"It's spilled milk, Kip. Don't be so paranoid."

Mark tried to manually play back the length of the tape on a small reel-to-reel at the workstation. He threaded the tape through the player's head with his fingers to see if he'd cut a perfect measure off the copy of the drum track.

"That's just going to take too long and it's too sloppy," Kip said. "Don't you think we may as well dump the sounds into the sampler, then fudge the part, and *then* edit the fudge *into* the track?"

Mark swiveled around to look at him. "That'll work."

Mark looked as if he'd been crying for hours; his eyelids were puffy and raw, his eyes veined. He looked old and pathetic. Mark attempted to smile, but it looked unnatural and disturbing on top of an expression that otherwise suggested heartbreaking misfortune.

"Are you sure *nothing's* wrong?" Kip said.

"Nothing that affects you personally," Mark said.

Mark called it a day early in the afternoon. Kip and Mark had fudged a drum track with the sampler but it sounded fake, contrived in the studio. That didn't work for the traditional rock and roll sound this band went for. Kip hadn't enjoyed the process either—the work seemed to heal nothing in particular, probably because it wasn't any good.

"Hey, Pop," Kip said. "Is it too late to call?"

"No, not really. Are you in jail?"

"No. . . ."

"Just had to ask."

"Are you doing OK?"

"I'm doing good. Treadmill's working." Kip's dad never failed to acknowledge a gift he had found useful and touching.

"Good to hear."

"Listen, I'm having some trouble at work. Maybe you can help."

"It's the gay guy, right? Mark?"

"Uh . . . yeah. . . ." It still stunned him to hear that from his dad. "He seems to be in some kind of trouble but he just won't say a damn thing about it. And it's driving me nuts. I just can't let go of it, Pop."

"OK. Does it bother you that he's in trouble, or does it bother you that you're not interested?"

"It bothers me that it bothers me."

"Maybe it's a homosexual panic."

"No shit," Kip said. "I've known him for a million years now, and that's not a problem. His boyfriend is a friend of friends, seen him awhile, don't know him much. It didn't bother me, it doesn't bother me. His boyfriend's an OK guy, from what I know. Honestly, I don't think about it that much."

"That's because you're not interested in it."

"Right."

"So what's the problem?" Pop said.

"Maybe I really don't want to know."

"Listen, there was a gay guy in the band—everybody knew it, no one talked about it. We felt a little sorry for him because he seemed not to be put together like the rest of us in the reeds. He was really talented, though. Eventually he got fired because he made everyone uncomfortable."

"Because he was gay?"

"No, because he was a basket case. We were all trying to do our job, and he kept screwing things up every now and then for reasons we never could figure out, and to top it off, it seemed he was about to fall apart every other week. We couldn't count on him. Same thing as firing an alcoholic or a junkie."

"Did you ever bother to fuckin' ask?"

"Ask what?"

"Why he was so upset."

"It was a different time. Now, don't get upset at me, we just didn't know back then, and probably still don't know. We bohemians were far more used to seeing it, though, so you can imagine we cut him a lot of slack."

"OK, Pop."

"Why don't you just ask him what's going if you want to know so badly? Maybe he just got held up at gunpoint. That shakes you up for a couple of days."

"OK. I'll call him."

Kip tried Mark's number and got the answering machine: "Hi, this is 212–555–3790, I'm not home at the moment, so leave a message and I'll get right back to you." He realized that *I'm* and *I'll* used to be *We're* and *We'll* not long before.

Kip went to work very early that morning and assigned himself a couple of studio hours that hadn't been leased from the twenty-four-hour schedule. All by himself, he managed to accomplish the work they'd abandoned the day before. Mark made his appearance on time.

"Been here long?" Mark asked.

"A few hours, more or less," Kip said. "I don't know, I thought I should fix the drum problem."

Kip played back a rough mix of that section of the song; he finalized the production on the drum track by disguising the synthesized parts with the use of a sound-effects box designed to distort electric guitars. It worked perfectly with the fudge, which otherwise sounded too clean and perfect, and he added an extra moment of trippy drama to the short sequence in the song.

"That's fantastic," Mark said. "Well done. Very well done."

"Thank you," Kip said. He still so much enjoyed impressing his pal. Kip picked up a clipboard and scratched off The Problematic Drum Track from their to-do list. "We're a whole morning ahead of schedule."

"Is that so?"

"I want to take the morning off. Let's go and do something. Let's not even talk about work."

Kip and Mark found a booth in the Russian coffee house; Mark ordered tea and Kip ordered freshly squeezed orange juice.

Kip chose the easiest way to put it. "I noticed you've changed your answering machine."

Mark looked at his tea; he lifted the glass to his lips, sipped, and put it down. "That's very perceptive." Mark settled his glass on its saucer and leaned forward to speak in a very quiet voice. Kip naturally leaned forward over his orange juice, then moved it aside in order not to spill it. "Dean just left me. He just left me. Didn't say anything."

"I'm sorry to hear that," Kip said. "Why'd he do that?"

"I can't tell," Mark said. "I really can't."

Kip struggled to respond despite his discomfort. "You'll have to forgive me, but I really hate it when you can't trust me."

"I can't tell, as in I don't know. It's weird. I don't know for sure but it looks pretty bad one way or the other. You know, Dean and I have been planning to get a house. It just happened that I got a weird rash a few weeks ago. I went to the doctor, and he counseled me to take an HIV test just to make sure it wasn't some kind of complication."

"Is the doctor a 'phobe?" Kip said.

"No, actually, he's gay," Mark said. "*I* asked him if it was a complication."

"Oh, shit, man. . . ."

"I told Dean about it and Dean said we should take it together. A few weeks later, he'd pick up the results. The day before yesterday, I get home from work, and I find that all of Dean's stuff is gone. And there's no note, nothing to explain what had happened. He just *left*. The day before he'd left me a note saying he had to meet with friends, and I thought nothing of it. I believe he must've gotten the results then, and he decided to leave me but he couldn't tell me."

"Why do you think he left you?"

"I think he left me because I'm sick."

"What a little shit. But you're not sick, right?"

"I don't know. Maybe we had a superficial relationship and he couldn't handle it. I don't know. I only found the envelope last night. Dean comes home earlier and picks up the mail. So I know that has something to do with it."

"Are you sure you're sick?"

"I haven't called to ask. My rash is gone, anyway."

"I'm sorry, man. Listen . . . whatever happens, I'm here for you."

"I appreciate it."

"I'm sorry," Kip said. "I'm really sorry."

"This is the first time any of my straight friends have asked me about my private life. I'm really moved."

"I'm sorry I didn't ask before."

"I didn't want to do this to you," Mark said. "I've been through some difficult times."

"Listen, don't you *ever* keep anything from me," Kip said. "I seriously hate that. It pisses me off. It confuses me. It makes me feel like I can't do anything for you."

"You really can't," Mark said. "I never thought you'd be interested."

"Bullshit. *Bullshit*."

"I don't think you can."

"Bullshit," Kip said. "You're going to get your results right now."

"Don't push me."

"Sure I'm pushing you. It's my job to be pushy. How is this different from any other time?"

"Because I don't want to know," Mark said.

Kip settled back calmly and went for his glass of orange juice; it slipped out of his hands and spilled all over the table. Kip tried to pick up the spill with the thin, small napkin he'd been given; it was a futile attempt at rescuing the moment.

"I need some time," Mark said. "I'll get to it."

"Let me know what turns up, 'cause I sure as hell want to know."

"Can we let it go at that?"

"I don't know," Kip said. "I don't think so."

The lady in the album collectibles booth eyed Kip patiently as he considered his options; she had brought the record down from the wall display at his request. Kip looked at the album, wondered if he could get away with this purchase without anybody questioning the expense. It would be difficult to explain to someone who didn't collect records, who didn't worship The Velvet Underground and/or Nico and/or Andy Warhol: a mint condition of the first edition, the plastic cover never opened, the vinyl never played. Its jacket had a peelable yellow banana. And it had never been peeled. The peel would come off to reveal . . . something. But at the price of stripping it of its full value.

A fellow shopper approached him with the look of someone hoping to ask for something he knows he shouldn't ask. Kip looked at the intruder as if he were a distant acquaintance at a funeral or a wedding or a launch party: the person seemed familiar, but Kip couldn't place the face or his relationship to it.

"I know, it's pink banana," the intruder said. "Are you buying that?"

"Hi . . . you're, uh . . . ?"

"Dean," he said. "We've been at a lot of the same parties."

"Oh, yeah—you're friends with Mark, right?"

"Sorta, kinda. Are you buying that? 'Cause I really want it."

"Nah, I was just looking at it." Kip handed it over to Dean. "I don't think I can justify buying it."

"Oh, I can justify it. I'm buying it so someone else won't have it." Dean took a money clip from his pocket and paid for the album in cash. "So, how's Mark doing?"

As the lady made change for Dean, Kip noticed that his money clip looked familiar. Kip had given Mark one just like it as a Christmas gift a few years ago. The lady bagged the album and gave it to Dean. Kip smoldered and grabbed Dean's arm before he went on his way.

"Why the fuck did you leave Mark like that?" Kip asked.

Dean pulled his arm away. "Why would you find that so interesting?"

"I work with the jerk every day and I won't accept or tolerate the grief you've given him."

"Is that it? Are you done?"

"No, I'm not done. Maybe he's sick. You can't just abandon a guy."

"You know what I hate about straight white people?" Dean said. "That the only way they can relate to something is if they can make it about themselves. You're making this story about you, and it isn't. What's it to you if he's sick?"

"But it's about me, too. . . ."

". . . I'm sorry, but I currently have *no* sympathies for the problems of straight people."

"How so?"

"Because you seem to have no sympathy for *mine*."

"I have *plenty* of sympathy. I can't stand to see him so unhappy."

"That's your problem."

"It's not just my problem. We have to have something in common."

"Well, we do have something in common. I can't stand to see him unhappy either."

"Is it because he's sick?"

"No," Dean said. "You don't understand. I'm sick. Not Mark. Mark's fine. *I* tested positive."

Kip didn't know how to respond. A sense or relief crept through his shoulders. Kip couldn't pretend to be interested in Dean's misfortune; it would be like betraying his solidarity with Mark, or his loyalty to his own emotions.

"Listen, they cured polio," Kip said, "it's going to be all right—"

"They haven't cured a fuckin' *thing* in *years*," Dean said.

"Hey, listen, my bad—"

Dean patted Kip's arm twice. "I'm sorry. I just don't want to hear this right now," Dean said. "Maybe another time."

Dean walked away, toward the cartoon collectibles. Kip stood there, by the record booth, trying to look at a vinyl album of easy-listening music on the table display. He could hardly concentrate on the one thing in front of him. The world had to be more beneficent than it appeared to be; he had to be a better person than he immediately felt like being.

But he wasn't interested. He couldn't make Dean's misfortune interesting for himself. He didn't want it to be interesting, or complicated.

Death by Bricolage

FALLING PREMISE

The cadaver, dead on Place de la Chemise, was found at
2:13 hours by a bunch of medical students and academy
painters on their way from a night of prostitution. The offi-
cials of the Sûreté called me to aid with the special investigation: I, Johnny Apollinaire, with my combined Doctor of
Philosophy in Crime Detection and Cultural Studies from
the Sorbonne, ordinary murders being the franchise of ordinary detectives, and extraordinary ones being mine—I
was also deeply broke and had friends in the office and
needed new shoes . . . anyway, I was called from easy
dreams of teapots to attend to the body because the State
Necrologist refused to slice up the defunct like so much
fromage since it would be akin to destroying an eternal
work of art for the sake of mere momentary justice. The
corpse was exquisitely covered with bits of paper cut from
newspapers, art catalogues, product labels, dissertations,
advertisments, manifestoes, comic strips, manuscripts, epi-
grams, laundry lists, form letters, love memos, café menus,
and Post-it notes, not one bit of skin left exposed to the
stank Paris summer atmosphere when it was found. And
in that state, I confronted that monument, transferred
from Place to Morgue, kept under a shroud of mystery
from the press. The press would make a big deal of it in the
morning paper, and by noon a million poems would have
been written about it, confusing the job of us poor slobs

who have to wrestle with the Truth. It was hot. I hated poets and I had to work fast before this mystery got to them.

DISQUISITION BETWEEN OTHERS

"It is indeed a death," I said, "beautiful or not is not the issue." The chandelier in the Morgue swung to and fro, casting shadows that would not stay still. I was sore from bumping my head into it.

"But it is lovely," said the executive secretary. "Is this the way you would go, Monsieur A?"

"One wonders about the necessity of such questions," I said. We had worked together before; I tolerated him only because I could boss him around, and he never asked me if I was related to *that* poet, or was *that* poet. *Quelle horreur,* being mistaken for someone who I am not.

"Well, won't you play with that question for a moment?" the executive secretary said. "I mean, if you were to choose your own death, how would you go?"

"We have hardly any time! The answer to this mystery before us could be of the utmost importance to France, not to mention the world! Imagine a world where deaths like this became commonplace; we would have no idea why they happened! And we would have no idea how to stop them." I was being dramatical for the purpose of impressing my importance upon the executive secretary, who was being far too casual to me about me. Alas, the executive secretary was deeply hurt, as if I'd slapped his face. He made big, sad portrait eyes at me, and I couldn't help but at least give him a half-assed answer to his question. "Well, this way is as good as any."

"Really? Wouldn't you want to die in your sleep? Or from some noble disease? I mean, this is a rather elegant death."

"Death by collage? It's no more elegant than pthisis. Is this a collage or a bricolage? I could never tell them apart."

"So much for your vaunted knowledge," said the executive secretary. "I thought that all distinctions were known to you."

"I am not here to be judged," I said. "Leave me to my work or just leave the room. I do not wish to engage any longer in spurious arguments."

"Well, damn you, what does the corpse say about its death, about itself, about us! I think the language of the collated images has something to do with it."

"Ah! The corpse has unusually large feet," I said. "Unusual enough for them to be traceable. Attend to measuring the feet and addressing every shoemaker in town. Feet this large cannot pass unnoticed. See what you can cobble with this factoid. You have until lunch. Get started. You might find me at Café Semblable then."

"But the images, the words! What do they say?"

"I doubt that Plum's Potted Meat or SPAM have any mimetic value," I said, inspecting the cadaver with latex-gloved hands. "The letters are written in purple prose and received ideas. The manifestoes are full of indifferent contradictions and blah conceptions. The Post-it notes are inane. There is no homicidal imagination capable of constructing meaning from such casually chosen signs. Broken guitars have more to sing than this."

"Ah . . . ," sighed the executive secretary, "I may be too Romantic for my job."

"You are too romantic, with a little R. It takes a mind empty of references, allusions, resonances, and connections to see things as they are. The world is sick, I tell you, *sick* with flecks of eternity and relevance, of importance and relation, of obsessions with some fourth dimension that is not there to be brought out from space and duration and memory and all that jazz, of goddamned *art,* for the

Truth to be really known. Now let me be with the body to observe it, unattached, selflessly, as if I were a ghost of Truth, unblemished by cultural nattering, and/or you."

The executive secretary bowed with hesitation, removed his pince-nez, which had one slightly chipped lens, and left the room, afterimages of his cretinousness and irrelevance in his wake.

CERTAIN REPRESENTATIONS EMBODIED

INNER BEAUTY KIWI FRUIT luminous photo of man with closed eyes *d'immobilité, d'éternité, d'incorruptibilité* A thousand household uses! you can't account for all experiences (unreadable Braille) MAN FOUND DEAD OF KNOWN CAUSES a three-dimensional postcard of the Blessed Virgin "Look behind you!" she said Liberation Sale, no payments before Thermidor mankind beats its drum, announcing the passing of an era NO SUBSTITUTIONS location, mediation, construct with mourning *remember to feed the cat, you bum* "that rare *thing . . .*" *Landscape with Lump of Meat* (5½ x 8, ink on paper, c. 1993) 2 shirts, 3 slacks, 1 handkerchief We EFUSE o live unde such unpomising culual consains as pesened by he alphabe . . . so, in poes, we EFUSE o use he lees T and R unil ou desies fo feedom of expession come o fuiion HISPANICS OVERINNOVATE *I will always love you, my little artichoke, but please vacate the premises* wafer-thin crackers the text, overdetermined, destroys its subject, you know angels with no angles SOME ASSEMBLY REQUIRED brains have a lasting appeal that looks only aspire to in the future, keep all memoranda to a minimum *Nude Lady Looking at Fruit* (8½ x 11, gouache on black velvet, c. 1988) POST NO BILLS Extra-Pep! folkpolitik on the lurk LES FRÈRES BOUILLION AEROSTIERS: Your Access to the World *Dear Mlle. La Chose, it so beau-*

tiful there is no market for it negotiations were disrupted by the appearance of MEANWHILE . . .

LUNCH

And so, after a morning of inspection, I bicycled from the Sûreté to my favorite café, to have a consommé devoutly to be wished, and a plate of spleen and plums. The café's specialties were elegant food made from unusual foodstuffs with much verve. This morning's specials involved dead twig salad and breaded bouncy deer steak with a side of *pain*. Alas, while I deeply wanted to eat and meditate, the sous-chef, an ex-lover of mine, sat down at my table. One thing I loathe about the sous-chef is how much he threatens to make my life about him. I am not interested. How could it be explained? I worship his little toes, I adore how he makes soup. But only the alone can see the Truth.

"I made the consommé thinking about you this morning," he said, "thinking it would rain."

"The clouds have yet not broken." I said. "Ah, why would I say that!? I have been indoors since six in the morning with some dead person, and I assume it has not sprinkled since the time I last saw the sky, as if it would only rain if I were there to see it fall, swiftly, to the ground."

"My window by the kitchen gave no evidence of such," the sous-chef said. "I just saw butterflies and bees dancing by, dancing for the possibility of our embrace, and of late all I can consummate with you is broth."

"Don't be pathetic," I said. "Bees have better things to do."

"How's the soup?"

"It's faboo. I am helpless with the desire to never reach the bottom of the bowl. But I will. Such is the fate of mankind."

"I will make you ubiquitous soup one of these days. Just you wait."

"What if there is no more water? Or chickens? Or farmers or rainclouds?"

"One can never know but hope."

"You are far too fantastic. I could only really love you if you weren't so flaky, and that's not in the croissant sense."

"You do love me, Johnny, you do. You love me because you love my soup. There, no more proof is needed."

"I hate having relations, I hate assigned meaning. I want to be known only for myself, not as the farmer's son or the sous-chef's squeeze, or even the false-fleck-revealer. Why must I be defined by what I perform? I am not a thing that is Johnny Apollinaire, the soup lover, the one who knows what's puce and what's lavender, who installs track lighting, who sings sea chanties in smoky cabarets, I want no genders, no names, no descriptions, no boundaries, I want to be me me ME! Or at least someone like me."

"You are frightening the customers."

"Then please leave my table. I want to be alone with my meditations and the soup that is now coming to its oblivion."

"But what about us?"

"There is nothing named *us,* no community, no conversation, no copulation. That was the past, banished, gone, nothing to remember us by. Rain has come! See, it melts our scripted past together. Ciao, toots."

"We'll always have soup," the sous-chef said. "Honest soup, the soup of us."

"Sentimental wretch! There are no more sincere gestures in a world exhausted by Irony. Begone with you, you have disturbed my uncompromised view of Life, passing by the café window, in the rain. What's for dessert?"

"Flan Rapture."

"Oh, call it crème caramel, you phony. Don't call it

something else to make it more exotic. You, you are as sick as everyone else!"

"It's YOU, you are the sick one, sick with pretensions of disconnectedness! All is related, resolute, complete, and you just cannot see it!"

"I trust nothing," I said. "Not even fragments, *mon cher.*"

I made the sous-chef cry, and he ran crying to the kitchen to cry into his soup. Would soup with his tears taste better? Alas, I could not chew that philosophical cud, for I had better things to think about. Poets, for example. I hated poets. Poets got on my nerves. Poets, those fleck-flacks with their whiny little voices and heads full of goddamn poetry, the way they position themselves as supreme distinguishers of difference and sameness, of the ordinary and the extraordinary, the ridiculous and the sublime, the something, the other, and that over there on the side of that other thing. It was poets who were to blame for the state of the world, with their revolutions and reinventions and mental unrest, how they imposed something of themselves on otherwise indifferent Truth, which neither asked for their intrusion nor needed it. A poet must be the murderer, no doubt, I thought; someone more practical could have done the deed with less pomp and circumstance. It would have taken years to accumulate all that debris stuck on the poor deceased, not to mention the impossible chore of mucilaging the corpse piece by piece with paper. Was it humanly possible? Perhaps not, but a poet certainly had that kind of patience and inhuman resourcefulness. I had to start thinking like a poet or the case would go unsolved. What Irony! Alas, the executive secretary arrived on a bicycle, a manuscript stuck under his armpit.

"I hope not to interrupt your meal," said the executive secretary, "but not only have we found the shoemaker who has made shoes that size, we have the appellation of the cadaver and we have found three living persons who were in contact with the deceased in the weeks before his untimely death."

"Untimely? It must have been timely for the murderer."

"That may be, but in any event, the authorities have tracked down the relatives and taken depositions."

"Without my presence?!"

"Sorry, but we had to work fast. Their stories might change by the time you met them."

"Everything happens when I am not there. I should have had some take-out."

FABLE OF THE DEPOSITION

The decedent's brother made the decedent a drafting table and a tall matching chair. Built them with his own hands, finished them with bright green acrylic, the vinyl table surface flat and angled perfectly, a large, matching lamp clamped on the top edge. They hadn't seen each other in a few months, since the day the decedent's employer dropped by the decedent's cubicle and told the decedent that it looked like it was time to take some time off from work. The decedent had to cram for the Architect's Certification test, which the decedent wanted to pass in order to execute visionary designs for his own architectural concern, so the decedent readily agreed; besides, he felt he had to make some time for a special project that he was bent on seeing through.

The decedent's back hurt from crouching over the flat desk that was stuck in the corner of the room in the clinic—not a good space on which to lay out the blueprints for the dwelling of his dreams. The brother's drafting table was a surprise, not just because it was precisely what the decedent needed, but because it was his brother who had made it for the decedent. The decedent was deeply touched. The decedent hugged and kissed the decedent's brother. The decedent's brother was stunned, he almost shook the decedent off. Feeling the decedent's brother's struggle, the decedent told the decedent's brother that the drawing table was not just a drawing table, it was sublime. It spoke for the decedent's brother, and the decedent wanted to respond to his brother. The decedent's brother then let the decedent hold him for a while. Soon the decedent's brother grew accustomed to the decedent's hugs, even to like them.

The decedent drew his brother a sports center in his castle so they could shoot hoops, swim, and play tennis together. He drew his brother a large carpentry room full of power tools and heavy equipment and an expansive, inexhaustible forest from which his brother could cut down trees to build the furnishings for the house.

The employer, the decedent's only true friend at work, brought the decedent drafting paper, rulers, blue pencils, and pens. When the decedent asked his employer for crayons and felt-tip pens, the employer brought them without question. Brought construction paper, but refused to bring X-Acto knives. The decedent's employer brought safety scissors instead.

The employer followed the development of the plans with interest, asked a lot of pertinent questions that helped the decedent visualize the concept, gave the decedent some suggestions on the design, though the employer expressed some reservations about its viability. The employer couldn't see a contractor building the decedent's castle, or how the decedent could send it to the sky, or how it could stay there. The decedent's anger bubbled up to his lips and he called his employer a Philistine. From then on, the decedent's employer never questioned anything. The decedent drew his employer his own section in the house, where the employer could have his computers and his drafting and maquette tables. The employer would have even a little artist's studio so *the employer could paint when he got tired of designing buildings, and a museum to display models, plans, and paintings. The employer was thankful and stood still as the decedent held onto him and told his employer he was welcome, until a nurse came in and told them visiting hours were over. The employer went home with the promise of bringing over a contractor to start talking costs.*

The next time the employer showed up with a watercolor he'd done of a cheap porcelain coffee cup floating in a vast, gray, and desolate seascape, empty but for a coffee spoon. It was the decedent's favorite. The decedent's employer had it framed and titled it I Have Measured Out My Life in Coffee Spoons. *The painting hung like an open window on the wall facing the decedent's bed. They talked about Gothic cathedrals and Ayn Rand.*

The decedent's girlfriend came to visit as well, and brought him plants, flowers, vegetation, a cozy, warm touch to the decedent's pad. The girlfriend read the newspaper to the decedent, discussed the engagement and wedding announcement pages in particular, and sneaked the decedent some Sylvia Plath.

The girlfriend made the decedent a crazy quilt to keep him warm. The girlfriend made him pajamas in dark purple silk, cut, sewn, and embroidered without the need of a pattern. The decedent wore them often, his body wrapped tight in all the right places, loose where his shape was flabby, an attractive tuft of chest hair peeking through the V neck. The day the decedent first tried them on, he beamed, took his girlfriend very gently, and cradled her in his arms. She played coy at first, then started to voice objections about their privacy and the neighboring rooms, which only turned on the decedent. The decedent lifted his girlfriend into the bed, asking her not to be loud so as not to wake up the neighbors, and he made love to her.

The girlfriend did not resist the decedent at all but soon she started to cry. The girlfriend cried quietly and the decedent pulled himself out from inside her and asked her what was wrong. The girlfriend couldn't answer. The decedent consoled his girlfriend by whispering how the decedent's girlfriend was going to have her own large garden to putter in inside the castle. How she would have a silkworm garden, with silkworms that would weave silk in every color in the decedent's crayon box, silk that the decedent's girlfriend would stitch together in her own airy, well-lit millinery. How decedent and girlfriend would share a huge bedroom in which they could make love and scream out loud all day and no one would hear them, not even the decedent's brother or the decedent's employer. Not God, who would live in the castle, in His own personal space, inside the cupola, which would be held up, by some grand mysterious plan of His, without a foundation. Not even anyone on the earth floating by underneath them.

ELABORATION OF THE INSCRIBED PATHOLOGY

"That soup looks good," the executive secretary said.

"What a terrible story! The *locus classicus* of the disease of culture."

"Very. Are you going to eat that?"

"I take it one of these three must have done the ill deed. This has all the signs of a mercy killing."

"What kind of soup is it?"

"Ah, seeing a perfectly sane architect gone sour with visions of grandeur must have been no piece of cake to live through. But which of the three is the most likely to have a grotesque imagination? The brother!"

"The brother was in one of the Paris communes, he was never alone. The girlfriend was at home, sleeping with the employer; you see, suffering unites the otherwise unrelated.

Besides, she is into architects. For this we have the landlady for corroboration."

And I am into chefs—shut up, brain. "Why isn't this in the report?"

"I thought the deposition had come to an aesthetically pleasing end. Is that julienned fennel floating there?"

"What? What is this crap about an aesthetic end?"

"Well, it was a nice place to end the report. Is that fennel?"

"Don't tell me you're a poet."

"Well, I only did not want to make it unreadable."

"How *dare* you express a poetic instinct in a purely representational medium! You enforced closure on the story! It should be arbitrary, like life!"

"What's poetic to you is representational to someone else. It also has a bit of ideology and eros in it. That *must* be fennel."

"Oh, that only makes it *worse,* doesn't it? Aesthetics and ideology! Eros! You poets are the end of my days! You cannot be avoided, can you? At least you did not try to slip some autobiographical narrative into it."

"Well, I did sort of identify with the deceased. If only slightly at first, because I will die, too."

"You have completely *contaminated* the case. Now we will never know who did it. You poets, you are everywhere. You are like germs hidden inside the cells of otherwise pure institutions, your poetry an unending murmur in the cultural conversation like a diseased heart's."

"Mix your metaphors, will you?" he said. "Oh, don't be so sore. The original recorded statements—we filmed them—are in the office for your perusal. We have plenty of other materials for your use. But, I promise you, there's not much to them."

"Really. So why did you waste my time? Why did you

come here and spoil my lunch? I will never understand you poetic types."

"What's there to understand?" said the executive secretary, discombobulated.

"Why make such a spectacle of yourself?"

"What kind of a stupid question is that?"

"That's it," I said. "I quit the case. If you and your Sûreté cannot play with untrammeled facts, with useful information, you do not need Truth, and you do not need *me*."

"I don't," the executive secretary said, chastened.

I threw my napkin down and left the café. I looked back as I wrapped myself in my mackintosh and put on my bowler, and the secretary was finishing my soup. The sous-chef came out with my spleen and plums, obviously looking forward to torturing me some more with cuisine, and was startled to find the secretary in my place. Then, with commonplace courtesy and goodwill, the sous-chef addressed the secretary regarding the oncoming main dish, and the secretary said he would eat it, too, and proclaimed that the soup was sublime. With this, the sous-chef sat down to talk with the secretary as if the substitution of the secretary for me in the logical order of things were an ordinary occurrence. I could tell by their googly eyes that soup was only the subtext of the conversation, and perhaps the lovely main dish would emit hot moisture until it was cold, and perhaps it would never be consumed. Indeed, what God would fabricate such a tableau.

That was no more a mystery. All of creation did not want to cooperate with me, who knew the Truth; the slippery world only trusted poets and thought only poets could see it. And then there was the corpse: no one would rightly know how he died and who killed him. God killed the architect, wrapped him in labels. Stuck with relations, the corpse could not negotiate with and reconcile into one consistent universe where everything fit in and no one or nothing was left out. Perhaps God favors, over all, poets, while it is I who should have been dead.

I could no longer watch this scene being performed for me. The bicycle had rusted in the rain, and I would have to walk home. The street vendors were out of umbrellas and sold only apples and sewing machines. I wandered lonely as a clod. I slipped and fell on my ass and died.

Ephemera

Summer night. Driving light slices the ceiling. They hold each other.

Are you comfortable?

Yes.

Long city walk, a kiss stolen quickly, fear of being caught.

I like this very much.

When exactly do you know you're in love?

Me too.

Mark serves iced tea, tall glasses, at home.

Funny, I keep thinking what to say.

Dean likes the taste. He asks Mark how he brewed it.

How so?

Ice melts. Half-full glasses on the kitchen table. Beads of sweat on the glass.

Well . . . what are *you* thinking? You always respond with a question.

How do you know when to kiss someone?

Actually, I am thinking the same thing. I thought you'd have an answer.

I don't.

You usually do, Dean.

What makes a couple a couple?

Are you really comfortable?

Oh, Mark, I'd hate to say just how amazingly comfortable I feel.

Why *hate?*

There you go again!

He is still there beside you. The folds and bends and lengths and furrows, the smoothness and hair have become familiar. The way he smells. The way he breathes.

All right. I'm very comfortable. I like holding you.

I like holding you, too. I like it very, very much. There. A no-brainer.

Phone calls. Dates made and kept. Movies, plays, concerts, dinners.

Can I play with your hair?

Go right ahead.

Your hair . . . your hair has such . . . body.

Don't make me laugh. . . .

It does!

Well, thank you very much, sir.

Summer night. Quiet, slight laughter. The feeling of a body against you.

If I said you had a beautiful body, would you hold it against me?

Dean. . . .

What?

Don't make me laugh.

I like that.

You have a nice . . . scalp.

Kiss it. Kiss it again.

Ticket stubs in pants' pockets. Visa bill in wallet.

You *are* trainable.

And you're a cute thing.

Dating weeknights. Long weekends together.

Don't you hate it when people won't talk to you after you fuck them?

You no longer notice when he turns at night. You keep a set of clothes in his apartment. He keeps a set in yours. Not being together is harder than not being apart.

Why *hate*?

Restaurant guide, listings, Playbill.

Oh, never mind.

Sit together, watch TV. Rent a movie.

What do you mean, people?

Could this happen with anyone else?

I'm only sleeping with you now. If you're wondering. I'm not.

Not that I was seeing anyone before you. Or at the same time.

Me either.

What does a couple look like?

What do you think after we make love? I always wondered.

Days pass by. Steal a moment. A murmur.

That I don't want it to end.

Are there words, gestures, objects that tell you what this is? You made it up as it went. How do you negotiate the unnamable? It's become so easy not to be alone. It's become so easy not to care if you're alone or not, but you'd rather be with him.

God, I wish it didn't.

Summer night.

You mean it does.

What do you expect?

Their hands folding infinite paper.

I'd like to fall asleep as soon as it's over. Not notice it's over.

Oh, you mean the making love. I thought you meant the dating.

No turning back. Look behind you: you surprise yourself with the notion that you are with this *person at* this *moment. You've lost count how many times you've made love. You don't know if he's going to die; if you're going to die. You don't know if you'd walk out on him, if he'd walk out on you. Maybe sickness wouldn't be the reason: career, unresolvable differences, fate . . . another man . . . a woman?*

Do you think we'll—

I really really, really like you, Mark.

How do you know that it's love?

It's hard to say.

I don't want it to be over. The dating. I could live without the fucking.

You don't——

Nononono I mean that the fucking pales in comparison with the dating.

Really?

Are you surprised?

You always surprise me.

Mark and Dean talking, making love.

I think I am falling in love with you.

Silence.

Me too.

You hold on tenderly to what binds you to this earth: your precious knowledge, the music in your head, your talent, your words, your toys and things: what you possess. Those would conceivably never leave you, would they?

It's starting to be a hassle. Having to make plans.

Hey, I plan my schedule around you.

I do too.

How do you know? How do you know?

What are you doing this weekend?

Let's see: Friday night, Mark. Saturday, Mark. Sunday, Mark. You?

Is it something that you know?

I'm doing Dean.

Hmm. Is there a pattern to this I can't perceive?

Objects can be stolen, music unheard, knowledge unused. Words never stay still. Words change you.

What are you doing tomorrow?

The usual. Prepping for the season's big Barbie doll convention.

You're kidding.

No. Not really into it. Not into girls' dolls. I'm not into stuff that's too popular.

Hope it's fun.

Lots of shipments and anxious owners. . . . A nightmare, a fucking nightmare.

When is it over?

Friday I'm banging the gavel. We're expecting a big turnout, though.

I see.

The big thing is I'm expecting a private collection that lists a Banana Splits lunch box. *That* I'm getting.

Someone selling?

Someone died. Awful to get first dibs on what the dead leave behind. . . .

You'll give it a home.

Words are ephemera. Talk is cheap. If you are as good as your word, what value do you put behind it? What do you mean?

I'm in the studio tomorrow. Recording.

How's that going.

I had Kip scream at the bass player for being late today.

Tight schedule?

They're coming unrehearsed. Too many takes. They're making it up as they go.

Oh, boy.

I don't know how anyone tolerates that. We're over budget.

Well, they get paid to be stupid and out of control.

That's unprofessional.

You have to take it.

I've worked with people who were stoned but on time.

Really?

I don't mind as long as it doesn't get in the way of my work.

I didn't figure you to be kind to that.

It's fucking everywhere, Dean. I do a little pot once in a while.

And you haven't invited me to partake?

You smoke?

Not really. I was just teasing you. Getting any work you like?

Oh, yes. I got another remix. Not a lot of money, but it's a big name.

Time you made a comeback. Make your own stuff again.

I'm fine where I am. I like what I do.

You know, you should remix the Banana Splits. They're due a comeback.

You're fucking kidding.

It would bring up the value of my soon-to-be lunch box.

Do you cherish them, collect them, number and store them where they will not be damaged? Or do you preserve and present them in a way that evokes muses? Are words music to you, do you precisely time their duration and tone their timbre? Is your conversation a sustained variation on the theme of you, or of you both?

There's a really greedy side to you.

Summer night.

Wouldn't you want what you care about to be valued for what you think it's worth?

I never think much about what other people think.

Their hands folding infinite paper.

Lucky you. It matters a lot to me. I wonder if I should give a fuck.

It's your business.

You certainly can afford not to care.

I do care. Just not that much.

I don't want the stock to fall on things I like.

My stock fell. I let it.

But your life wasn't over.

Will yours be?

If you stop talking, do you stop existing?

I could lose a lot of money if I made the wrong decision.

I know a lot of people who did, you know.

In music?

Yes. Who had nothing to fall back on. They hang around bars now.

If I didn't have my work, I'd think myself dead. . . .

There's more to you than the auction block. Or your collection.

Well, if you couldn't work because no one cared about you, how would you feel?

There's carpentry. I'd still make music for myself.

Things fold neatly into place, like a well-made map.

I wouldn't know what to do. What I do depends on other people.

Who do you talk to when you talk?

There's me.

I should just give up and run a small collectibles and antiques store.

There's me.

You know for sure you are avoiding the real issue. You know what it is, you know what you want, you know what words to say, what to propose, what to ask for. You hope that subtlety works in a way that directness might not. Is this subterfuge just a way out of committing fully to what you feel? Is the strategy what makes it work? Is there a quality, a pleasure, a flirt, a seduction to this game?

I mean, what would I do with all my shit if I couldn't sell it?

We could move to a bigger apartment. Or a house.

Cosigning a lease. Packing, moving, making space.

What do you mean *we*, kemosabe?

We make love again. God knows where the energy comes

from. God knows what our future is. But there is one in front of us. Our words made it. We cast the spell. We will let others know, we want others to know, so it's as real to them as it is to us.

We say this is us, not only you and me, we.

What's your current value on the market?

Has-been pop star. Not much to me now. You still love me.

Yes. I think I'm going to keep you.

I love you, too.

You better put that on paper.

Summer night.

You dog.

The right word is *bitch.*

Their hands folding infinite paper.

Fixing a Shadow

i.

It all started with a dull discomfort, followed by a feeling that he would explode at any moment, but then nothing happened, and then Bob strained for something to come out, but it didn't. Once in a while a burst of liquid would accompany the strain, but mostly it was an uneasiness, and running to the bathroom, and nothing happening, but he felt he could force it out. Bob went to work anyway, it shouldn't get in the way of having to make a living, a subsistence he needed, if not desperately. He stuck it out drinking soda and soup. It might have been the street vendor's chicken sandwich, or the sponge his roommate forgot to keep dry, it might have been that he'd been abducted by aliens not altogether expert on anal probes, but of course that last possibility he could have enjoyed, too, like he enjoyed the sandwich and the roommate, if they'd done it right, and maybe they'd have let him remember it if it happened. Or he would have remembered it anyway, in spite of the pangs of guilt such pleasure would bring to Bob, since as far as Bob was concerned, he was married, you know, to his roommate, to someone he loved but he didn't want to bother with the complete details of his food poisoning and hold-it-in-push-it-out stiff-lower-rim colitis, except that when they'd had sex over the weekend Bob had to declare this area out of bounds. So Bob and Bradley just smooched and fondled and mutual masturbated and it was good. But holding it and forcing it began to hurt, too, but hurt differently, like something had been gnawed down there. Bob will head to the hospital emergency room. It's getting bad, he'll shit blood, but first he has to go to work.

The photograph shows two men in a kitchen. The kitchen's cupboards are blond wood with a slight finish that throws a diffused glow, a reflection of what once was the camera's flash (which accounts for the subtle halo surrounding the subjects). The countertop has the odd dish, pot, and pan. Apparently a meal has occurred involving the two subjects, and dishes are being washed. It used to be that snapshots represented qualities by how they captured people, that they could read good and evil in their subjects, as if features correlated with behavior the way symptoms correlate with disease. They have lost this quality now, photographs; a picture is worth a thousand words, but that's only a *very* small dictionary.

More unease and weakness and dullness and crankiness. Bob changes the background screen behind the square, fluff-carpeted table where a small boy sits with three dolls his father has handed him to keep him busy. The backdrop, blue like milk mixed with food coloring, rolls down with a whir.

"I want the full set. . . ." the father says. "Actually, scratch that, how about the four portraits and twenty wallet-sized. . . . Wait, what, what other choices do I have?"

You mean, starting with whatever child support leaves you, Bob thought, nodding, accepting the fact that this customer believed his thoughts would interest a chain-store photographer; they did, but Bob wouldn't expect this to be reciprocated. God, was he a mean bastard today. Poor kid with a deadbeat dad, this is what you'll have to remember by when you're all grown up, a Sears photograph. The child, with slicked-back wet hair and overalls and a red stripy shirt and new black booties, holds the furry blue doll with the cape and the helmet and the chest insignia.

"What were the—you know, how much is it again?" the father asks.

Criminals have simian features and defiant turns to lips and eyebrows. Needy people have hungry eyes and over-eager smiles. Lilies are sexy. That's not very much! How the value of photography has cheapened! What took one photograph now takes a battalion of photographers to render in one day's worth of shuttering, and even then they sheepishly admit they missed something. According to one urban myth, too many photographs have been taken and now the visual holds back its enchantments. Like someone sore from discourteous stares, it has become, not invisible (if it had it wouldn't *be* itself, if there were such a thing), but *ineffable*. In any event, I still have the photograph of the two guys in the kitchen, and I still can't figure out the one whose appearance I associate with disease, and I can't figure out why the one washing the dishes is looking at him.

"The price list is on the counter," Bob says. He can't quite frame the boy and the three dolls. It's too cluttered. The father wants it that way, but does the kid really need all those dolls?

"Well, you know how it is, you walk past the booth and you want to have your photo taken," the father says. Funny how subjects often confess or apologize to Bob about something, as if having their photo taken had something to do with their lives, as if, if they did not say anything that seemed personal and intimate (or that passed for it), the photo would not come out right. "Maybe *I* should get a glamour shot, huh?" the father asks. "Well, maybe not for me, but I need something to show to other people, or they might not believe I have a kid. I mean, everybody has something to show for themselves."

"Three dolls?" Bob asks neutrally.

"Just one then," he says, "he likes Super-Grover."

"Who doesn't." He leans down to smile, wide-eyed, at the kid, before taking Ernie and Bert away to the toy hamper, more discomfort in his stomach. "Just the one, sweetie." Bob sincerely wants to appear friendly to his subjects, especially children, but he does not want to violate their proprietary feelings about themselves (or their parents) or appear inappropriate in his interest.

One man, with his back to the camera, is turning his head to face the other man. His profile is too perfectly posed, and his expression (quiet curiosity, I surmise) seems too clearly directed toward the other man while he is washing the dishes. It's odd that one man would look at another man *this* way, don't you think?

The boy doesn't make a grab for Ernie and Bert, but smiles at Bob as if he were amused by the attention being paid to him. Bob Koehr is good with children in the portrait studio; a small comfort since most of the business involves children—children and teenage couples. Bob tells himself that though he might never have his own kids, he at least gets to photograph them, but this no longer bandages anything. An unfinished degree in art therapy and Montessori lies in state in some filing cabinet at a nearby university. In a carton file box in the apartment he shares with his boyfriend, Bob keeps assorted tax forms from a series of employments that had, outside of his ability to fulfill their job requirements, only a passing acquaintance with his real, if blurry, interests. So he used to work at an auction house and at an art supplies store, where he met

Bradley. At first it always seemed that each job was ideal, that he knew enough about it to do it well, and each job always paid better than the previous one, but just enough to live over the poverty line. But since Bob and Bradley split the rent, it wasn't that bad either, but not so good that they didn't worry about it on occasion. Most of all, Bob took jobs that wouldn't make him take work home with him. But of course, he did bring something with him: they made him think differently, or made him think about what it was that the job presented to him—objects of value, art materials, kids. Kids seem like the ideal goal; no, not like a goal, more like a hope, a hope of . . . of what? But what else is there but to have kids? And what was it that he could have with Bradley, since they couldn't have kids? Dogs? Cats? What are they both for?

The other man, leaning against the countertop, looks straight into the camera (I could say unflinchingly, as if he feels he is facing something that calls for valor if not defiance) and he looks sick, but not very sick. Kind of thin sick, like all the substance has been sucked out of him—maybe by the camera?

"Why do you think kids like dolls so much?" the father asks.

"I don't know," Bob says, turning to the viewfinder, pulling focus and adjusting the frame smoothly, with a practiced movement—now that it was down to one doll it was easy. "I guess they like them 'cause they resemble them; big head, big eyes. . . . I guess they like to see something that resembles them. Have you shown him a mirror? Kids will look at themselves for hours and hours and laugh and giggle. . . ." Bob turns to see the father looking down to the counter price list.

"Shoot the works," the father says. "His mother is getting half of them, anyway."

"All right," Bob says. So much for kids and dolls. Bob looks at the child and thinks, I could give you a mirror. He thinks it for no reason, a flash of thought that makes no sense other than that it pops into his head like a resonant phrase, and the kid stops and stays still as if stunned. And at the moment he connects with the child and grins and the child lights up instantly with a kind of bearing that seems full of surprise and life and joy and character, Bob presses the trigger and the camera snaps.

Bob's stomach cramps inside him, a serious cramp which says, *Pay attention to me now*. What timing.

ii.

In the hospital emergency room they pump out Bob's stomach with a tube, waves of everything he's eaten in recent memory flowing out of him into a bedpan. Bob can't help but roar, as if the gut sounds and the mush were of the same material. Although the plastic pipe down his throat is frightening and uncomfortable beyond his experience, it is a purging desirable to the point of being pleasurable. And so he roars louder and more shoots out of him, until he is empty and peaceful inside. He is so dehydrated and weak now that they stick an intravenous feed in his arm. They tell Bob it was a miracle he held on so long in this state and ask him to sign the admissions paperwork, which he looks over carefully, like a menu, as if he's figuring out what he feels like eating and what he can afford to eat. They want to keep him for a few days to see what the internal bleeding is about. Bob thinks of calling Bradley and a few other friends to tell them where he is hospitalized.

It seems the second man, the sick man is not looking into the camera, but at something inside the camera, perhaps something on the other side, or something through the camera, through the photograph, looking out as I am looking in, perhaps looking behind me? When people look into cameras, do they look at something inside them (inside themselves, inside the camera), or at the photographer, or at me, looking at the photograph on the other side. This is not like finding true love. This is inevitable. Does he look something *into* it, into me? Will looking at him make me sick, too?

An Asian nurse comes to give him an enema and then test his colon for blood with bits of tissue like litmus paper. She asks Bob to turn around on his knees on the bed. She tries to slip her gloved hand inside Bob. She has some trouble taking a sample, and Bob's confidence in his body control is shaken.

"Don't worry, I won't stimulate you," she says, like a schoolteacher.

There is an old man, quiet, sleeping, on the other bed in the room, curtained off.

"All right," Bob says quietly, and he relaxes, and she sticks in and swabs one strip of paper, then another.

"Here are some more strips," she says, handing them to him. "When you have a movement, take a sample, but don't hurt yourself."

"I can do that." The tissues are in a small package, like paper matches.

Now something curious happens! I look up from the photograph and catch the waiter looking at me looking at the photograph of the two men in the kitchen. He stays there, looking at me, as if I were an object worth perceiving, and for a moment I am, still lost in the picture. I do not want to embarrass him and quickly take the two-cup French press and fill a third cup (Guatemalan, sugary, half-and-halfed; I'm a little teapot, short and stout). The waiter dives behind the counter, but being gazed at so benevolently (he looked at me with gentle interest, I can safely assert) does not violate my privacy at the table. I love (dangerous verb) being looked at this way, and I look at the photograph of the two men again, in this mode of being. I want you in me, I want the me you see inside the me in *me*.

"Are you gay?" asks the doctor. Bob thinks the doctor is cute in a nice-Jewish-boy kind of way.

Bob thinks how does he know; why does he have to ask; how gay am I; how sick am I.

"I should say so," Bob says. "Why's that important?"

The gastroenterologist sighs. "Look, I'm a doctor."

"Well, I want to know."

"I'll be straight with you." He snorts. "Did you cut your-self with a blunt object?"

"What?"

"OK. Did you shove a broken bottle up your ass?"

"No. . . . Jesus, what do you take me for?"

"Sex toys? When was the last time you had sex?"

"Only last weekend. And it was just a jack-off."

"Really."

"Yeah."

"Did you get fingered?"

"No," Bob says. "Look, it's not like my asshole is the only part of me that makes me gay."

"I'm not asking for this."

"No, but this's what you're saying, right? And why does it matter if I'm gay or not?"

"Colons don't just start bleeding by themselves."

"So? It has something to do with me being gay?"

"Essentially."

"My asshole, right?"

"Isn't this all there is to it? Anal sex? There isn't anything else to it. Now will you tell me what you did to yourself?"

"You and I know I ate something that made me sick,

and I have not been able to shit for days, and when I did, I really had to push it out, 'cause I'm tired of being sick and I want my life to go on, and I think I broke something down there doing it."

"Have you gotten fisted? Ever?"

"No, I've just gotten fucked with a normal, ordinary penis."

"How big are your partners."

"Oh, please. He's . . . *regular* sized. Look, I'm not very patient, and I'm working on that. Now I know I shouldn't just push it out on my own."

"M-hm?"

"I think if I'd puked it all out like I did today I would have felt a lot better instead."

"Well, you're very lucky," the doctor says.

"Fine," Bob says.

The doctor pats his leg sympathetically. "I'll drop by tomorrow, OK?"

"Sure."

You press the button, we do the rest. The photograph is in black and white, small grain, slow speed, with high contrast, and the framing has the feel of someone who knows how to look. If I were its photographer, could I think of a better way of framing it? What relation would it portray, imply, infer, from a farther distance? Hmm. A well-appointed kitchen; master cabinetwork; clean, attractive, functional appliances; gas stove; frost-free fridge; two guys. How about from closer? Washing dishes in a sink, gentle on your hands. Hands gripping, gripping a countertop being leaned on. Hold a second. These guys are together. Just how together are they? You're soaking in it.

The hospital does not get cable, but the television buzzes anyway, unwatched. Bradley comes in with a change of

clothes, the tattered old orange workshirt Bradley knows
is sort of a security vestment for Bob, a sketchbook and
drawing supplies and a stack of paperbacks, detective fiction, comic fantasy, near-future science fiction, magic real-
ism, the whole nine yards. Bob doodles, skips through the
books. As soon as he gets bored with one, he jumps to the
other, he's too restless to focus on one thing for long. But
it was good to see Bradley, and maybe he should have
asked him to stay longer. The old man in the other bed,
closer to the window, doesn't say a thing. The light runs
through the curtains around the old man's bed, making
it gossamer, like a slide, like a stained-glass window, and
the man doesn't acknowledge Bob, or Bob's roommate, or
Bob's other visitors, friends who bring food and under-
wear and magazines and stay and chat and play cards. The
old man doesn't get any visitors himself, he just lies there
dreaming into nothingness, until he speaks to Bob on the
second day of Bob's stay.

"Have I done well by you all?" the old man says.

"I'm sorry?" Bob says.

"Have I done well by you all? Have I done well by you?"

"Me?"

"Yes. You and everyone else."

"I think so."

"You think so?"

"If not, I would have noticed. And said something."

"Oh, good, good," the old man says.

Bob thinks: Apparently the old man thinks that I'm his
son or something.

"Do you know that I love you?" the old man says.

"I never doubted it." I never doubted it: strangely, Bob
blurts this out and he's surprised that he means it, because
he does. He's not pretending for anyone's benefit.

"Because I do love you. I want you to know this."

"I know," Bob says.

"Could you turn down the television, then?" the old man asks.

iii.

Bob has gotten well enough that he can eat what passes for mild solids, and then they keep him from eating for twelve hours so they can send a scope up there to see him from the inside.

"This is probably going to make you uncomfortable," the doctor says. A nurse and another doctor stand in vigil while Bob reclines sideways on the table, his left leg slung up on a stirrup.

"I can take it," Bob says.

"Just let us know if it it starts to bother you." They lubricate his rim with some cold, plasticky unction and slip the camera right into him. At first it's a familiar sensation, and Bob gets a little worried that he does find it stimulating. But soon he feels the cable being guided deeper into him, the instrument making dull whirrs and clicks as it follows the contours of his innards, and it's like having a metal snake enter him and clumsily find its way around him with sudden sharp aches that he tolerates enough to keep quiet. The staff executing the procedure stands behind his back. Bob stares forward at the operating-room wall, wondering what they're looking at, and then the camera inside him stops moving.

"Can I have a look?" Bob asks.

"Not just yet. There it is," says the gastroenterologist. And the doctors and the nurse murmur to one another. Apparently they have found what was broken. "Now, Bob, we're going a little further in, this might startle you."

"I'll let you know when to stop," Bob says. So the tube with the little mirrors and rotors and lenses travels further into him, and it is unpleasant, and then it is flat out torture. "Ohhhh-K!! You can stop now!"

"You're a good sport, Bob," the Doctor says, and they pull the instrument back for a second or two. "You can look now." He hands the instrument to Bob. Looking through the viewfinder, Bob sees a slick, pink-freckled, ridged surface adorned with green globules.

"Cool," Bob said.

They draw the camera back down to his colon and show Bob a gaping wound, now healing.

The photograph is untitled, unexplained to me. Some photographs see print with dissertations attached to them. A certain photographer is known for one photograph (another one, not this one) and the countless exegeses that adorn it, some his own, some written under pen names, some by best friends he coerced into signing or fleshing out, some by people who hardly know him, some by people who just wanted to jump on the bandwagon, and now the photographer is no more and the industry just won't stop writing about the single snapshot, a single child with many relations, although the MLA and GLAAD have issued statements against its study as heinous and an unsuitable subject for discourse. Apparently, one photograph was all the photographer could take. The photograph absorbed so much energy, like a black hole, that this was all he could produce, and then comment on and revise and print and reprint and reuse. The T-shirt of the snapshot remains a best-selling item at Village T-shirt, postcard, and poster shops, outselling all the other applications of the negative, even the drink coasters and place mats. This is all I know, its history. I've never seen the photograph—said to contain the last and possibly truest insight into gaiety, relationships, AIDS, and the nature of art—and probably never will now, since terrorists (everyone claims to have burned it, and no one knows who really did it) have silenced its negative permanently, and all I can say is extrapolation on anecdotal evidence. Copies from copies, digital restorations, and even fakes keep being passed around in secret, but I refuse to see anything but originals. But I do have this other photograph at the moment, in my hands. I shake it a bit to see if the two guys in it move or tell me something.

Bob pays off what his insurance doesn't cover from his hospital stay. As he heads to the elevator, it opens. A man is rolled out in a wheelchair by another man, and neither of them look like hospital people. They are familiar to him, though.

"... I can walk," Dean says.

"Let me just roll you out," Mark says. "I like it. I enjoy it. Don't you?"

"Dean!" Bob says. "I mean, Dean. . . . Fancy meeting you here. Where've you been?"

"Well, Bob! I've been around. Sort of," Dean says. "This is Mark. What are you here for?"

"We've met," Mark says. "We've met a few times." Handshake.

"Good to see you, Mark," Bob says. "Oh, nothing special. I just ate something wrong and I dealt with it the wrong way. You?"

"Well, Mark and I are moving down to Puerto Rico soon, and I just wanted a battery of tests before we move. The doctor who knows me best is down here, so we came here, I mean, we've lived upstate for a couple of years now. . . . I can't believe we lost touch! This is *so* embarrassing. Look at us, we're like old people talking about what ails us."

"People drift," Bob says.

The two guys are mute witness to my frustration with them. But if it's frustrating, it's got to be good. Nothing worse than something easy to get. So boring, so superficial, so blah. If I read the gaze of the one washing up and the one gazing at me, well, what all-seeing eye appears in the geometry of our relationships? I see them together in a significant way, but in a way signified by them and me together. I am significantly other to them. Or at least this is what the photographer wants me to think! I think I am being set up. Tricked, suckered, bamboozled into interpreting something from the photograph. But I am not so stupid! I can understand this photograph better than the photographer intended. And yet the guy staring at me looks at me defiantly (no, you can't take me!), the guy washing dishes looks at him in the way the waiter looked at me (you are interesting and beautiful—dangerous adjective—and I look at you, so you are mine). I feel so other, I feel so left out! Why are these guys together? I want to know them from the inside out, and this photograph won't let me.

Funny how Bob never stops having feelings for Dean. They are different now, but they are still there. And it's a strange measure of his maturity, at least to himself, that when he sees Mark and Dean together, he doesn't feel jealousy or rancor. And he never did, even when Dean took him to meet Mark at lunch, and then Dean asked him what he thought of Mark, because Dean and Bob had become close and Dean wanted Bob's approval. And Bob had wanted to introduce Bradley to Dean, but they had lost touch by this time.

"Won't you come up for the weekend?" Mark says. "Dinner?"

"Dinner, definitely." Dean nods. "Bring a friend with you if you like. We have plenty of room for you to stay. . . ."

"Seriously?"

"Oh, we love having guests, don't we, Mark?"

"That's what we're all about."

"You gotta be about something," Bob says.

For the moment, Bob is about Mark and Dean. Bob wants to be about something, always about something, and this week he has been about being in the hospital, as he has been about other things in the past. And he will be about something else in the future. But there is something about Mark and Dean that always intrigues him, and perhaps this is why he feels the way he feels about them, that what they are is something to be *about,* something to be *for.* And now this something is something that Bradley and he are, too, or at least Bob imagines this is true, and he thinks that he wouldn't be who he is if it weren't for Mark and Dean. They were the first gay couple he'd ever met. Here's looking at you. I could give you a mirror.

"Hey, I've got an idea," Bob says. "I'd like to do photographs of couples. . . ."

"We are *hardly* representative," Dean says. "Like we're going to be poster boys for the Happy Gay Couple Foundation."

"Fuck *that,*" Bob says. "Who cares about that shit? Why don't I take your photograph? It would be fun."

"Nonononono," Dean says. "I'm not questioning your idea, I'm questioning your choice of *us.* Can't you do better?"

"I think I'd look fine with a whip up my ass," Mark says. "We'll do it."

"Well, maybe just one photograph," Dean says. *"One."*

"This is very sweet of you," Bob says.

"Isn't Bob such a Grover?" Dean says. "It breaks my heart. God, I hate having my photograph taken."

"Don't worry," Bob says. "It'll be a good one."

Or at least a metaphor for what I think is you, and please pardon my hubris that I can metaphorize you, since metaphors are not real, only an approach to people and things, and more often than not crass generalizations that have nothing to do with your essence, if there is such a thing. But I've got to start somewhere. Sometimes you start with the ghost, sometimes with the house, but there are no ghosts without houses, and no houses without ghosts.

in order of appearance, more or less, special thanks to

The Álvarez Foundation for the Arts (Papi, Uchín, Lyvia, Nuria), Mike Chase, Mary T. Helmes, Norman Finkelstein, Mike DeSeve, Jim DeSeve, Bradley Brown, Ron Kolm, John Pavlou, Madison Smartt Bell, Steve Bard, Simon Black, Bernice Mast, Stan Flukinger, Alex Kelly, Susan Minot, Paul Allman, Alisa Kwitney, Scott Smith, Amanda Filipacchi, Tom Beller, Frank and Jean Cipriani, Whitney Krueger, Micheal Brodbeck, Ted Kessler, Julian Kaiser, Al Peters, Jane and Michael McDonough, Luisa Fuentes, Finnegan, Ron Helpman, Thomas Farrington, Natalia Aponte, Greg Cox, Madeleine Robins, John Ordover, Rob Stauffer, Katherine Kroeber, Kim Kindya, José Nieto, Glenn Hauman, Hazel Trock, Jo Laine Gee, Paul Chirumbolo, Sheryl Fowler, Gail Whittier, Pauline Kaldas, T. J. Anderson, Virginia Shirley, David Chirico, Michelle Moore, Steve Zani, Frederick Garber, John Vernon, Susan Strehle, William Haber, Jim Gardner, Deborah Artman, Deborah Atherton, Andrew Kaplan, Mark Ebner, Emily Nussbaum, Carol Bly, Will Kolb, Ed Vega, Susan Koppelman, Gary Bellomy, Bernard Cooper, C. Bard Cole, Jarrett Walker, Brian Bouldrey, David Waggoner, Linda Eisenstein, Doug Lawson, brett josef grubisic, D. Travers Scott, Hugh Coyle, Sarah Schulman, Sarah Messer, John and Jodee Rubins, and Don Glauber.

About the Author

ALDO ALVAREZ has an M.F.A. in Creative Writing from Columbia University. His short fiction has appeared in *Blue Penny Quarterly/Blue Moon Review, A & U Magazine, Christopher Street,* and *Best American Gay Fiction 1* (Back Bay Books), among other periodicals. He is the founder, executive editor, and publisher of *Blithe House Quarterly: a site for gay fiction* (http://www.blithe.com). As a Clifford D. Clark fellow, he received a Ph.D. in English from Binghamton University.

Aldo loves to receive e-mail at ADAlvarez@aol.com.

Interesting Monsters has been set in Old Style No. 7, essentially a "modernized" version of the classic Caslon type. Its lineage goes back to a face cut in the middle of the nineteenth century by the Miller and Richard Foundry of Edinburgh, Scotland. That face, in turn, engendered another old-style face cut in the United States by the Bruce Foundry in the 1870s. This version was cut by the Linotype Corporation in the 1920s.

This book was designed by Wendy Holdman, set in type by Stanton Publication Services, Inc., and manufactured by Bang Printing on acid-free paper.

Graywolf Press is a not-for-profit, independent press. The books we publish include poetry, literary fiction, essays, and cultural criticism. We are less interested in best-sellers than in talented writers who display a freshness of voice coupled with a distinct vision. We believe these are the very qualities essential to shape a vital and diverse culture.

Thankfully, many of our readers feel the same way. They have shown this through their desire to buy books by Graywolf writers; they have told us this themselves through their e-mail notes and at author events; and they have reinforced their commitment by contributing financial support, in small amounts and in large amounts, and joining the "Friends of Graywolf."

If you enjoyed this book and wish to learn more about Graywolf Press, we invite you to ask your bookseller or librarian about further Graywolf titles; or to contact us for a free catalog; or to visit our award-winning web site that features information about our forthcoming books.

We would also like to invite you to consider joining the hundreds of individuals who are already "Friends of Graywolf" by contributing to our membership program. Individual donations of any size are significant to us: they tell us that you believe that the kind of publishing we do *matters*. Our web site gives you many more details about the benefits you will enjoy as a "Friend of Graywolf"; but if you do not have online access, we urge you to contact us for a copy of our membership brochure.

www.graywolfpress.org

Graywolf Press
2402 University Avenue, Suite 203
Saint Paul, MN 55114
Phone: (651) 641-0077
Fax: (651) 641-0036
E-mail: wolves@graywolfpress.org

Other titles from Graywolf press you may enjoy:

The Risk of His Music by Peter Weltner
Celebrities in Disgrace by Elizabeth Searle
Glyph by Percival Everett
Graveyard of the Atlantic by Alyson Hagy
How the Dead Live by Alvin Greenberg

CENTRAL

DATE DUE

APR 0 3 2002			
JUN 0 3 2002			
AUG 1 0 2002			
OCT 0 1 2002			
NOV 0 9 2002			
GAYLORD			PRINTED IN U.S.A